Jake Istenhegyi

THE ACCIDENTAL DETECTIVE

Nikki Nelson-Hicks

Third Crow Press

Third Crow Publishing
Gallatin, TN 37066
www.nikkinelsonhicks@gmail.com

Book Layout © 2016 BookDesignTemplates.com
Cover art by Jeffrey Hayes, www.plasmafiregraphics.com
ISBN 978-1-7349343-0-4

A quick word to the Reader:

Well, here we are.

The last three stories in Jake's New Orleans adventure plus a quick teaser for what I plan for him in the future.

Thank you all for coming along with me on this journey.

It's been on long, crazy, weird, zombie chicken filled ride.

Let's get on with it.

Nikki Nelson-Hicks, October 2020

CONTENTS

JAKE ISTENHEGYI:

THE ACCIDENTAL DETECTIVE

Fish-Eyed Men,
Fedoras and
Steel Toed Pumps

Many people ask to be victims in stories but only one person has ever asked me to make her a Hero. I dedicate this book to my sister, Melinda Paige Nelson. I hope your alter ego is as bad ass as you dreamed.

CHAPTER ONE

My Silent Partner

Morning hasn't cracked across the sky as I stumble back to the Odyssey Shop. I'm covered in blood. Not all of it is mine, for a change. I guess it's a check in the win column, right?

Not that it balances all the checks in the loss column.

I scrape a chair across the patio floor and sit beside the only person in this lousy world who will listen to me without judgement. Not that she has much choice, really.

Giovanna.

I trace the ivy growing along her arms and I leave behind a fat bloody smear across her marble skin. I try to wipe it off with my shirt but, no luck. It is soaked in blood and I turn a small smudge into a crime scene. "Sorry. Yeah, I know," I say to the serene, smiling face. "You can't take me anywhere."

She is the only surviving Lombardi sister. If one can call metamorphosing into a statue living. It's a drawback of the Sal Vitae Aeternam. The Salt of Eternal Life. The same stuff rushing through my veins. Miss a dose and you end up a planter in some bastard's patio. My poor, beautiful Giovanna. My reminder of my own fate if I don't find a new source of the Salt.

"Is it tomorrow yet?" I ask and wait a moment, more out of courtesy than expecting a response. "I don't know the time because I lost my watch. You're not going to believe this," I lean closer and whisper into her ear, "but a giant fish monster ate it."

I wait for an incredulous response. Again, only out of politeness.

"No, seriously! This morning, I had it on this wrist, right here, a brand new…well, not brand new but it was nice…well, maybe not nice but it was dependable and it was *there*, right there on my goddamn wrist until a few hours ago when, out of nowhere, this huge fish monster sucked it off my wrist like an oyster on a half shell."

I try to run my fingers through my hair, but it's matted with blood. Head wounds bleed like fountains. I lean in, resting my forehead on Giovanna's. I feel warmth where we touch. Am I feverish? I lick my dry lips and whisper, "You're not going to believe this. I can barely wrap my mind around it but, dammit, it was real. All of it. Not that I can tell anyone. If I do…if I had the balls to go upstairs right now and tell Bear everything that went down on the beach…tell him where Melinda is…try to explain what happened to Samuel…even if I showed him the goddamn journal…see?" I pull it out of my jacket pocket and hold it up to her. The strange leather feels obscene to me now. "Melinda let me keep it as a souvenir. It explains everything but, still, it wouldn't matter. It's so fantastic. Nobody will ever believe me."

I sigh at the bloody smear left on her forehead. I lick my thumb and try to wipe it away. "And I thought I had family problems…"

Thieving SOB

I woke up, confused, half naked and twisted in my sheets. These days, sleep is more like falling into a coma. What day was it? How long had I been out? I cast my memory back to the last thing I could remember before collapsing into my bed.

"Oh…my…God…"

….and the memories came flooding back.

The swamp, the rats and the relic hidden inside the pirate ship of Rameau, the Pirate King of Honey Island that held a shard of the Sal Vitae Aeternam. And, for a few moments, I had it… I held it in my hand! It was the last, hope of creating the elixir that would save me until it was stolen by that bitch, Henrietta Harleaux.

My gut boiled with a sick, acid rage at the thought of her. I thought she was dead, her body consumed in the same fire that took the body of my friend, Bear Gunn. But no. She had found a way to cheat death by using her own granddaughter as a vessel. The bitch should have stayed dead. When I find her again...and I would find her, this I promised myself…she would wish she had stayed in Hell where she belonged.

Still, on the bright side, there **were** the gold coins I pocketed while being held captive in the pirate ship. Worth, who knew how much? Hopefully, enough to pay off all the debts that kept me hostage to the shady partners of the Odyssey Shop and maybe a little something left over to buy myself something pretty.

I looked over at the stacks I had lined on the dresser.

"What….the….hell?"

I jumped out of bed, dressed only in my skivvies, and stumbled to the dresser. There was my wallet, flat from lack of any money. A comb. A pocketknife. My Bulova wristwatch. A thin layer of dust. Nothing else.

A cold thought rippled through me.

Radu.

Radu, my newly discovered half-brother had come all the way from Hungary to deliver a message from our mother, a woman I barely knew. After playing postmaster, he asked to stay awhile before heading off to California where he planned on becoming the next big Hollywood Movie Star. And like a chump, I let him stay.

I slammed open the pocket doors separating my bedroom from the living area he had been using to store his luggage. It was empty.

That son of a bitch.

I ran out of my apartment, down a flight of stairs and over to the landing that overlooked the store downstairs. Below, I could see Mama Effie sitting in her throne behind the cash register. Two of her loyal goons sat in overstuffed chairs beside a bistro table. One of them read the paper while the other one picked at his fingernails with a penknife.

"Where is he?" I shouted down at her.

Mama Effie turned in her chair and lifted her face to address me. She was graceful, thin and all angles, very much like a black widow and just as poisonous. She always dressed as if she was royalty and, let's be honest, in the confines of the Odyssey Shop, she was Queen. Today she wore a long-sleeved red rayon dress. In her closely cropped wavy dark hair she wore a matching rose shaped hairclip dotted with red glass jewels. She smiled and her teeth shone like pure ivory against her dark skin. She reached out her spidery arm and tapped her chin with a pointed, blood red fingernail. "Who are you looking for, *Boss?"*

She loved to dig at my public persona as the boss of the Odyssey Shop when she knew damn well that I was just a pawn. I kept my tongue. It was my best attack against her baiting.

"Radu. Where is he?"

"Somewhere between here and Hollywood. He finally settled on a stage name and set off two days ago."

"Two days? I've been asleep for two days?"

"Sorry, *Boss,* I didn't know you wanted a wakeup call."

My mind reeled in anger and confusion. "But how? He didn't have a car."

"He took yours. He said you wouldn't mind." She nodded at her goons. "The boys here helped him load the boxes."

I pounded my fist on the railing. "Son of a bitch!"

She waved a cream-colored envelope. "He did leave you a letter."

I went downstairs, taking two steps at a time. Mama Effie's seat of power was in the middle of the Odyssey Shop, a fortress of four waist high walls where she sat in the center. She arched an eyebrow and smirked as I took the envelope from her. Inside was a brief note on thick, crisp stationary:

> *Dear Janos,*
>
> *Consider it an investment in the future of a rising star.*
>
> *Look for me on the Silver Screen!*
>
> *Your brother,*
>
> *Jake Everett Powell*

Jake Everett Powell.

JAKE.

The bastard even had the balls to steal my name.

"I'll kill him." I said as I crunched the paper in my hand.

"Why? Did he run off with your clothes too?"

"What?" I felt a chill on my bare legs. Humiliation spread as I realized I was standing there in only my underwear.

Damn.

"Perhaps you should go get dressed….*Boss.*"

It took all I had not to bolt up the stairs as Mama Effie and her goons burst out laughing.

*****

Back in my apartment, my bladder confirmed what Mama Effie said.

Two days. Gone. Losing days was starting to become a habit. It was the Salt, the immortality elixir in my blood. I guess it worked best when I was asleep.

I washed my hands, cupped the cold water in my palms and splashed my face. The shock made me take a deep breath and I got a good look in the mirror. I was a mess. My hair was a crazy black halo. My cheeks appeared hollowed out, shadowed with dark stubble. But my eyes scared me most. They were empty, just dark holes in my face.

Jesus, what is happening to me?

I could still hear the laughter from downstairs as I hurriedly dressed in dark slacks, a white undershirt and a light blue button-down shirt. I picked out a pair of black socks and slipped on my Oxfords. I slid my comb, pocketknife and wallet into my jacket pocket and slapped my watch around my wrist. The leather band needed to be replaced but it kept perfect time. I almost put on a tie but decided it was overcompensating.

Besides, Bear never stood on formality. And what I was planning was best done on the sly.

Barrington Gunn Investigations rented the apartment below mine. I owned the building so, technically, he was a tenant, but he was also my best friend.

He was also a ghost trapped inside the Odyssey Shop. And I was the one who had put the bullet in his head.

I knocked on the door before opening it. The room was dark, so I reached in and felt the wall for the light button. "Bear? You here?"

No response. A dark sinking feeling dropped in my stomach.

We discovered he could leave the Odyssey Shop if someone took possession of one of his beloved *Black Mask* magazines. They anchored him. We never figured out the hows and whys of it. "Ghosting didn't come with an instruction manual, Jake." he would say.

The last time I saw Bear Gunn was a few days ago, after a brawl over in the Irish Channel. When he was alive, nothing got his blood pumping more than a screaming fistfight. He was having the time of his life, pun unintended, but the exertion took its toll. Afterwards, he was like a fading radio signal. And then he disappeared completely. I worried he might not ever come back. Can ghosts run out of juice, like a battery?

Closing the door behind me, I went over to his desk, opened the drawer where he kept a loaded .38 revolver, took it and a handful of bullets. I slipped the .38 into my waistband.

More boys lose a nut that way...

"Shut up, Bear." I muttered at the memory. I opened the bottom drawer where Bear kept the petty cash box. Inside was a roll of bills. Business had still been good for Barrington Gunn Investigations thanks to yours truly. Nobody knew the man in charge was so longer among the living and we kept the charade going with me doing all the legwork.

After peeling off a few bills, I had a think and took some more. I needed the money to find my thieving, bastard brother and afterwards to hunt down Henrietta Harleaux. It wasn't stealing, not really. It was an advance. Besides, what was money to a ghost anyway?

As I closed the box, I heard a woman behind me yell, "Thief!" and fireworks lit up behind my eyeballs as she walloped me on the back of the head

I went down hard, my head bouncing off the disgusting grimy carpet on Bear's floor. I tried to get to my feet, woozy as hell, but then the steel toe of a stiletto pump kicked me and slammed me into the dark.

CHAPTER THREE

The White Witch

The pain of being scalped pulled me back into consciousness.

A woman twisted a fistful of my hair as she pulled my head back and screamed into my ear, "Who are you?!" She slammed a knee into the center of my spine and I felt a steel toed pump drilling into my kidney.

"I'm Jake! Get off me!"

"Hello, Jake." She yanked my hair, pulling my head back so far that I heard my neck crack. "Where is Barrington Gunn? Tell me! Or I swear to God, I'll rip your eyes out through the back of your head."

"I don't know!"

"You're lying!"

"If you're looking for Barrington Gunn, esquire…" a gruff voice said. "Maybe you should take a gander behind you."

"Bear!" she said, releasing her grip on my hair. My head bounced off the floor and I grunted as she used my back as a jumpboard.

"Hello, Melinda, how's tricks?"

"Damn, you look good! What kind of hair tonic are you using?"

I groaned and rolled over to get a peek at my abuser. She was tall, even from my vantage point on the floor, around 5'9" and that's not counting the three inch stilettos. She wore a white skirt that reached an inch past her knees and a matching double breasted top with long sleeves and broad shoulders giving her a odd military bearing. She was fair skinned, brown eyes and a round face accentuated by her stark white bob haircut. She was attractive with curves Betty Grable would kill for, cupid bow lips and, to top it off, a cute snubbed nose. By the way she was smiling at Bear, she was definitely a close associate.

Death was an improvement for Bear. When he died, he was nearing his mid-fifties and his hard luck life was carved in his face. Death trimmed twenty years off the old WWI veteran. His face was full and his hair was thick and blonde and his fashion style was sharp as a tack. However, looking closer, I could see the illusion had flaws. He was fraying on the edges, like a photograph bleached by the sun. Further down, I noticed something more shocking: he had no feet. His legs stopped at the cuffs of his Italian slacks.

The woman went to hug him but he deftly slipped out of her way, sat down and settled behind his desk.

She held the gun out to Bear. "Here's the gun he stole from your desk," she said, frowning. His avoidance obviously stung. "He had it stuffed in the back of his pants like a regular rube. I thought you would've taught him better."

"Kids. They never learn. Put it on the desk. I'll take care of it later. Jake, are you going to lie there all day looking up her dress or what?"

"What?" She kicked my leg. "You dirty dog!"

"Ow! I wasn't!" I felt my face redden and I sputtered out my defense but I knew it would be useless. Bear would find a way to twist my words like taffy, making me seem more like a sap. It was best to shake it off. "Good to see you, Bear." I said as I got to my feet. "I worried you had taken another *sabbatical*."

He nodded and laughed. 'Taking a sabbatical' was our go-to excuse to explain why he would disappear, quite literally.

"It was touch and go there for a while, Jake. Touch and go. How about you? Did you get that Mallone problem sorted out?"

"A little yes. A lot no."

Bear raised a thick eyebrow at me and squinted, as if trying to read between the lines. "We'll debrief later but, for now, let me introduce you. Melinda Page, this is Jake Istenhegyi, my partner. Jake, this is Melinda, a former partner, crack shot and definitely not a woman you want upset with you."

"That much I gathered for myself," I said, rubbing my neck. "Hello."

"Sorry about the crack on the head. And for stepping on your back with my heel. And pulling your hair. And screaming in your ear."

"That's enough, children," Bear said. "The last scuttlebutt I heard, you were overseas, Mel, defending all the furry, feathered and scaly citizens of the world."

She put her hands on her hips and cracked a wicked smile. "Poachers the world over quake in fear at the mention of La Bruja Blanca."

Bear laughed. "The White Witch. That's precious. What do you want with me? I'm not in the animal business."

"One of the things I've learned while traveling the world is there are all kinds of animals." She paced and her eyes took on a shimmer. "I have seen things, Bear, some I never imagined existed…or could exist. Fantastic creatures."

"Okay, let's not get dramatic, doll. What can I do?"

Melinda Page sat on the corner of Bear's desk and leaned forward. Bear leaned back whether to get a better view or to avoid temptation, I couldn't tell. "I need your help, Bear. I have a client in need of your specialized skill."

His face blanched a bit and I worried he was going to fade out completely. "I don't do that anymore. Not since Bannerman."

"Bannerman was different and this time….I swear, Bear, it won't go all pearshaped. I'm desperate. My client is running out of time. There are dangerous people. It goes deep, Bear. Deeper than I can tell you. I need your help to disappear."

"Disappear?" I asked.

Bear waved my question away. "A different time, Jake. A different me. A me you should remember all too well, Melinda."

Melinda Page leaned back and sneered. "I should've known. I hoped you'd be the same Bear I knew way back when. The guy who fought alongside me against the Baron and the nasty case with those Bug Boys. Remember?" Bear nodded and his eyes glistened as he remembered. "But now…this is where you put down roots? The Odyssey Shop? You're no rube; you know what goes on here. It breaks my heart."

Bear stared at her, his eyes heavy lidded underneath his thick eyebrows. "Tread lightly, Mel a lot of things have changed in fifteen years."

"Not with the bastard owners of this…," her voice shook in anger and she spit out the word as if it were vinegar, "… *shop.*"

Bear nodded at me. "Present company excluded, I'm sure."

Melinda faced me and her eyes flashed. "Are you one of *them*?"

I put my hands up, palms out. "I inherited the building, much against my will, might I add. I'm only technically the boss around here. Trust me. Ask anyone. There's no love lost between me and whoever is the real brains behind this place. What do you have against them?"

"They are the ones hunting my client."

CHAPTER FOUR

The Partner Card

"Hunting? You need to be more specific, doll." Said Bear.

"It's easier to explain if you come with me, Bear."

Bear shook his head. "Sorry, sweetheart, no can do."

"But, Bear! Please! Once you've seen what I've seen, you'll understand."

"Sorry. I'm swamped. Take Jake."

"Who? Him? Does he even shave yet?"

"He's got a baby face but he'll get the job done."

"I don't know." Melinda squinched her snub nose. "He's kind of runty."

"Hey! I'm standing right here."

Bear laughed; he loved watching me dangle. "He does most of my legwork these days. It's the best deal I can give you, doll. Take it or leave it."

"Fine! I'll take him." Melinda threw her hands up, defeated, which did nothing for my ego. "Keep up and don't slow me down. Let's go."

"Not yet." Bear stopped her. "I need to debrief him on a certain matter. Write down where he can meet you and

I'll send him as soon as we're finished. I'm guessing we're doing this on the pro bono plan?"

"Let's call it a payment on a tab you've been running for years." Melinda rolled her eyes as she scribbled something on a pad, ripped the page out and handed it to me. "See you later, Jake. Bring galoshes, if you have them."

"Okay…wait, what? Galoshes?" I asked but she was gone.

"Yeah, she does that." Bear said.

"Who is she to you?"

"An old friend. When I first set up shop after the war, she was my secretary."

"Secretary? I didn't get the feeling she was much into steno."

"She was a better shot than stenographer, for damn sure. She started her own business and took up the good fight protecting all the birds and beasts of the world. She was always a sap for a furry face. Used to bring in strays and stash them in my office. I had every kind of critter crapping all over the joint. Now, take a seat, kid, and catch me up to speed. Did you get things sorted out with the Irish?"

I took the chair across the desk from Bear, just like old times. "It's all sorted. I don't think I'll be invited to any St. Paddy Day parades but I'm square with Brannigan."

"I don't know if anyone is ever square with that mick. He got back the money and the right joe that killed his fighter, Mallone?"

"Check and check. Mama Effie delivered the money so Brannigan's bosses won't be pressing on him. If he still has a beef with me then I'll deal with it as it comes. As for Mallone's killers, they are all dead."

"Killers?"

"It's a long story." The grisly memory of the reanimated corpse of Joe Katzimmer tearing two people apart is not something I wanted to revisit. Not sober, anyway. "It's sorted and that's enough."

Bear settled back in his chair and pulled at his moustache. "So, why did you need my gun?"

"Radu."

"What? That show pony? I know you didn't like the guy but what kind of beef requires a bullet?"

I told him. The words rushed out of me like bile. Everything ran together. The pirate ship, the treasure, Harleaux's return and how she used Pearl's body as bait to kill me in revenge for what happened at the barn. I told him about how everyone in Crabtree's treasure hunting crew was dead...or at least I assumed they were. About the Boodaddy, the protective talisman Crabtree had given me and how it had manifested into a creature made of mud, leaves and whatever detritus it could pull from the swamp. How if there wasn't a Honey Island Swamp Monster lurking around before there was now. I told him of the Salt and how I had it...*I had it in my hand!*.... but it was stolen by Harleaux. Stolen, like the gold that was going to get me out of the hole my family buried me in at the Odyssey Shop.

"How do you know it was the real stuff?"

"I could feel it. I don't know how else to explain it, Bear. When I touched the crystal...it's hard to describe. *It knew me.*"

Bear stared into the distance, thinking.

"And then there's this final slap in the face."

I tossed him the crumbled ball. Bear smoothed it out and a sly grin broke across his face as he read the note. "That, my friend, is one cold fish of a brother."

"I'm not the only one he screwed over. He told Mama Effie about you."

"How do you know?"

"She let me know when she said she hoped that no *kisértet* found there way in the store."

"Kisértet? What the hell is that?"

"It's a Roma word. It means ghost. It's what he called you when he saw you do your disappearing trick, remember? Just trust me. Mama Effie knows your secret now."

Bear shrugged. "It was going to happen sooner or later. Information is that woman's bread and butter, Jake." He tossed the letter into the trash. "So, it seems to me you are at a crossroads. You can either jackrabbit after your brother, hope he has your money and get it back. Or you can hit the trail while it is still warm and track down Harleaux and see if you can get the Salt. You can't do both."

"Why not?"

"Whichever trail you take is going to leave the other one too stone cold to follow."

The truth in his words hit me like a hammer in the gut. "Shit."

"I wouldn't get too bothered about it. Either way is going to end in a dead end."

That piece of news did nothing for my digestion. "How do you figure?"

"Well, the way I figure it, Radu...or *Jake*," Bear smirked at my expense, "will have found a way to convert the gold into some hard cash by now and knowing his taste in fedoras and frills, it's not going to last him long. As for Harleaux." Bear's face grew hard at the memory of her. In Bear's heart, she was his murderer even if I was the one who put the bullet in his brain. "Who knows where she is. Who was the buyer for the Cross of Trismegitus? Where is the buyer? West Coast? East Coast? Hell, she could've left the country."

"So, you're saying I'm screwed either way?"

"I'm saying you need to stop and think this thing through. And while you are thinking, stay here and help me with this case."

"Bear, we've talk about this before."

"I don't expect you to stay here forever but I need you, Jake. At least until I get back on my feet?"

"You mean, until you *get* feet?"

"Aw, hell. You noticed?" Bear shook his head. "It's taking all I have to keep myself this solid. I'm like a balloon with pin pricks all over it. I can feel myself leaking. Can you put all the other stuff on hold and be my partner for a bit longer?"

"You bastard. Had to play the partner card, didn't you?"

"I play the hand I'm dealt. I need you, Jake. Just a while longer."

"Fine. Go and do whatever it is you ghosts do. I'll check out Melinda's case and report back but when this is done, I'm going, Bear, one road or the other. I have to…"

And Bear was gone.

"…go."

CHAPTER FIVE

The Family Bible

I took the .38 and checked to see if it was loaded. It says something how easy I am around guns these days. Four months ago, I'd have been all thumbs. *Jesus, has it only been four months?* Back then I was the pen and paper guy. I stayed behind, did the soft research. Bear did all the hard P.I. work. I pocketed the gun and took a deep breath before going downstairs to run the gauntlet of heckling between me and the front door.

There were no customers, as usual. There was only a maze of shelves with all sorts of useless, dusty junk. The only real housekeeping done was by a kid, Mikey, who swept the floors once a week for a quarter. It was all a façade anyway. The more inhospitable it appeared to the outside, the easier it was to keep the rubes out.

Mama Effie was totaling figures from her ledger book. One of her two goons was napping while the other one read a paperback he must've pilfered off one of the shelves. I made it to the door when she said, "Going out?"

I ignored her.

"Dress warmly."

Her goons burst out laughing.

I could feel the heat of her toothy smile burning into my neck. I let the door slam as I left.

Since Radu helped himself to my car, I had to take a cab. And since this case was definitely going to go on the books as pro bono, the cost came out of my pocket. All of which did nothing to help my mood.

I gave the address to the cabbie. We drove by a surprising number of people for a Tuesday afternoon. Christmas shoppers, I figured. The sky was sapphire blue with only a few cloudy imperfections and the temperature was mild . How many days until Christmas? I only had one name on my list. What do you buy the ghost who has everything?

The cabbie dropped me off in front of the Sun Coffee Shop.

Damn.

"It all comes around to a circle, doesn't it?"

"What?" said the cabbie.

"Sorry, talking to myself." I paid the cabbie and tried to look harmless. "It's an occupational hazard."

The Sun Coffee Shop. This was where Bear and I were supposed to have breakfast on my past birthday. He had the whole day planned. A greasy breakfast, movies and then dinner with some dames he had lined up for us. We were going to paint the town red, he said. The only thing red that night was the barn as it burned down with the bodies of Bear Gunn, Henrietta Harleaux and a hundred demonic hell chickens inside. I am still conflicted between revulsion and hunger at the smell of roasted chicken.

The bell above the door jingled as I opened it. Two men sitting at a table near the door playing chess stopped and peeked over at me. I nodded and they went back to figuring out how to steal each other's rook. There was no sign of Melinda Page. It wasn't a big place with half a dozen tables, each with a pair of wooden chairs. In the back was a long counter with ten empty stools. On the wall behind the counter were posters of popular films and advertisements for hair oil, cough tonic and supplements to enhance a man's vigor and stamina. On the end of the counter was the French press coffee machine and, my God, it was a thing of beauty. A large round brass monstrosity that made my mouth water from the memories of the coffee houses of Paris. I walked to the counter with a renewed sense of purpose and ordered.

"You are a man who knows his coffee," said an old man in a stark white apron and a blue piped white paper hat. He was Old Country, through and through, and the hat did nothing to Americanize him one bit.

"Bon jour. Ça va?"

The old man wiggled his hand. "Comme ci, comme ça. Café?"

I nodded. My stomach rumbled. When was the last time I ate? "And a ham sandwich."

I sipped the coffee and my blood perked up. This was heaven. My heartbeat quickened as the caffeine soaked into my bloodstream. I turned to find a table near the window to watch for Melinda when I felt a tug at my sleeve.

"Are you alone?"

It was her. She had changed into a pair of white slacks, leather boots and a white leather jacket. I nodded and followed her to a table. She sat with her back to the wall and kept her eye on the window, watching the street outside. There was a nervous energy around her she didn't have before in Bear's office.

"I didn't see you when I came in."

"I was already here, watching you. Do you have any smokes on you?"

"Sorry. No."

"Damn." Her eyes darted on something behind me but I didn't take the bait.

"Say, between me and you, is everything on the level with Bear? He seemed...odd, different, kind of empty."

"He's fine. The lighting in the office is bad." I took a bite of my sandwich and another drink to let the lie sink in. "Besides, not everyone is as good looking as me."

Melinda laughed. "I'm being silly. My nerves are frazzled."

"So, what is up with the La Bruja Blanca?"

She smiled at the name. "I've always hated people who bully those without a voice, so I became their voice. The White Witch has caused many a man to stain his trousers, I can tell you."

"I have no doubt. What exactly are you protecting now?"

She took a deep breath and bit her lip as something caught her eye. I finally gave in to my curiosity and gazed over my shoulder. There were three men in trench coats, standing on the corner, sharing a match.

"Problems?" I asked.

"Maybe. They've been following me for the past two days. Your guys?"

I arched an eyebrow. "If you mean Odyssey Shop guys, I have no idea. My loyalty is to Bear."

"Either way, finish up. We need to get this show on the road. My car is round the corner."

I inhaled the sandwich in two bites and tossed back rest of the black brew. I grimaced as it scoured my throat. I followed her to the back of the shop. She slipped two silver coins to a black man pushing a broom and he opened a side door leading outside.

We ran down the alleyway for a block and then up another street, keeping as close to the backs of buildings as we could, until we stopped by an ancient, tortured Packard. The white paint was pockmarked, and the fenders were dented. If it were a horse, I'd be tempted to shoot it.

"I see you are as rough on automobiles as Bear."

She shrugged and got behind the wheel. "Cars are tools and tools are meant to be used."

"Used but not abused," I countered. A sour, fishy smell hit me as I opened the car door and sat down beside her. I noticed the back seat had been removed and there was a stained blanket on the floor.

"By the smell, I guess it's some kind of rare, expensive tropical fish the Odyssey Shop has a buyer for?"

"Oh, no. Samuel is a man." She looked both ways twice, pulled into the street, her eyes fixed on the road. "Technically."

"Technically?"

The sky was clouding over, making it darker sooner than usual so she turned on the headlights. I rolled down the window, glad for the fresh air.

"Reach under your seat." she said.

I did. I felt a leather bag and pulled it out. Inside, I found a thick journal bound in a grayish bumpy leather. I ran my fingers over the bumps and felt strange electrical tingles. "What kind of skin is this?"

"I don't know and I don't want to find out."

The book was bursting at the seams with yellowed papers and photographs. The only thing keeping it together was coarse twine tying it shut.

"It belonged to Samuel's family. Goes back generations. Imagine it as sort of a family Bible handed down from father to son. Open it."

The knot was too tight to untie so I cut the twine with my pocketknife. Freed, the journal sprang open and the pages blossomed like a bouquet of brown and yellow leaves. A black and white photograph fell out. I picked it off the floor. There was an image of a family standing on a rocky reef, near a lighthouse. The mother held tightly to her young child, a boy if the short pants were a clue, and with the other hand she cradled a baby. The father stood behind her, but his face was smeared like a dirty fingerprint.   I figured he must've moved while the photographer was snapping the picture.

"Which one is Samuel?"

"The boy. The baby is his sister, Rose. She was killed shortly after this picture was taken."

I made a sympathetic grunt and flipped to the first page of the journal. It was undated. The paper was fragile and felt like leaves in late autumn. I worried the pages would crumble as I turned them.

"See those ribbons? Start there. It begins with Samuel's father's entries."

There were several sections bookmarked with colored ribbons. I stopped at a black one and read,

'May, 1898. It took all my will to enter into the abhorrent thing but, the third oath is fulfilled.' The handwriting was scratchy and the ink was a strange ruddy color.

'June, 1898. The nets were full! As promised.'

'March, 1899. The boy was delivered to me on this day. He has been anointed Samuel. I have sent for a wife. She is young, not of our kind, fresh blood from Oklahoma. Amelia is her name.'

"I don't understand how this is pertinent to what you want Bear to do?"

"You need to know where Samuel came from to understand why he is so special. Flip to the gold ribbons. That's where Samuel's story starts."

I turned to a gold ribbon. The handwriting changed, a much steadier hand took over and the ink was darker.

'*April, 18, 1922. Brother Obed said my father wanted me to have this journal but forbade me to read the earlier pages. According to him the Norcutt family line is 'A lineage to be treasured and honored.' His exact words. He said the book was a family archive and each man of our family had to record his transition when he entered the Order.*

I was anxious to meet with my father since I had not had any contact with him since my mother stole me away to Oklahoma but I haven't been allowed to see him. The brothers all say I can see him after I have taken up the two of the three Oaths.

I've never had a diary before. I don't know what to say. I suppose it's like writing letters to your future self. If that's the case then, hello, Samuel! Welcome home! To the village of Morley, your birthplace. Can't you feel it? Here on the coast, for the first time in your life, you can actually breathe. Truly, freely breathe. The dry plains of Oklahoma never suited us...'

'*April, 25, 1922. I have begun the Oaths. The first two were simple enough. There was an oath of secrecy and then an oath of loyalty to the Order. To be honest, I felt silly wearing a gold crown and reciting words that made no sense. But Brother Obed says the Third Oath is not so simple. We shall see.*'

I flipped a few pages.

'*....after Mother's death I left home and wandered, eastward, following the Voice. I never told Mother about it; my nightmares always worried her so much I can't begin to guess how she would have reacted if I told her about the songs the Voice sings to me. Mother was a frail thing. I loved her but I always had the strange feeling she was afraid of me for some reason. I was glad to leave...*'

"He never knew Amelia was not his birth mother?"

Melinda shook her head and furtively glanced into the rearview mirror. "But Amelia was his mother in every other sense. After his sister was sacrificed, she escaped with him and fled back home to Oklahoma."

"Wait....what?"

"Go back a few sections. I have it marked with a red ribbon."

I flipped back and the handwriting was ruddy and scratchy. '*The wife has borne a daughter. A pureblood, fair and fat. The tide is low and the moon is high. Brother Obed tells me it is an omen. The girl is a good tithe.'*

"What the hell does he mean?"

"Long story short, they dangled her over the cliff, slit her throat and chanted as her blood gushed into the waves below."

"Krisztus! Why?"

"Read on."

A few paragraphs below there were the words: *"The tides were high and the nets were full."*

"With what? Fish? Are you telling me the girl was murdered for fish?"

"Fish and a few gold trinkets."

"That's barbaric. What sort of people is your Samuel from? Why do we want to help this guy?"

Melinda's knuckles were white as she gripped the steering wheel. "Flip back to Samuel's story."

Today, I could visit the hospital where my father is being treated. He has a dangerous skin condition so he was covered head to toe in wet sheets. Only his face was spared. I am ashamed to say I barely saw a resemblance between us. Except for the eyes, maybe. He strained to reach out to me but the wet sheets restrained him. I could see the outline of his arms; they seemed like horrible stumps. Had he lost his hands? I returned the gesture to comfort him but wasn't allowed to touch him.

I was excited to tell him about my completing the first two oaths and I was preparing for the third. He reacted strangely. His eyes grew wide and then he became angry, biting and snapping at us, until he convulsed on the bed like a fish out of water. When I commented on it, Brother Obed said it was a symptom of his disease. "Involuntary muscle spasms." My father tried to talk but his voice was garbled so Brother Obed played translator. Brother Obed said my father was proud of me and he always had faith I would return to him. There was more but Brother Obed said my time was close and I was taken back to my rooms to prepare for the third Oath. I am so nervous but there is no one to talk to. I am glad for this journal. It must have been a great comfort to my father...and his father...and on and on.

Oh, God. I am tempted to read the earlier pages of this book. Get a peek at what to expect but I fear it would be like opening Pandora's Box. I don't want to lose my father's trust. In a few hours....I can wait a few hours more...'

The light was fading and I squinted to read Samuel's handwriting.

I stood near the reef and listened to the Song. It is so strong here, so pure. More proof I am home. Brother Obed says the Song I hear will lead me to my true bride. Yes! That is the Third Oath. I am to be wed! In the same manner as my father and my father's father. It is the way of the Order, to keep it pure and to keep fortune shining on the town. I am told our brides come from the sea. From another island? I don't really understand. Brother Obed says the voice I have heard all my life is my one true love. She is calling me home.

Amelia was never my true mother which explains so much. Why she stole me away, I'll never know. What happened to my mother? I'll ask my father when I see him after the ceremony.

I am so nervous but I can't let the others know.

"A wedding?" I asked.

"Of sorts. But I doubt you'd find any church that would honor it. Remember what was in his father's section of the journal? Go back to the black ribbon."

I flipped back and reread the words: '*May, 1898. It took all my will to enter into the abhorrent thing but the Third Oath is fulfilled.*'

"Wait...what?"

The boy was delivered to me on this day. He has been anointed Samuel.

"I don't understand. What thing? Am I missing a piece of the puzzle?"

"Are you familiar with....no, I doubt you are. There were drawings of it throughout the earlier parts of journal. Take a look if you want but, I don't recommend it."

I flipped to the front. The pages felt crisper, more like leaves. The ink grew fainter and strange, briny smell wafted as I turned the pages. I didn't dare lick my fingers. I came to a sickly yellow page I could feel ridges from something had been forcefully etched onto the other side.

"Before you turn the page, Jake, think how much of the truth you want to know. How deep are you willing to go?"

My fingers trembled as I turned the page. There was a crudely done drawing. The ink was reddish brown and the page had a strange smell, like copper with a fishy undertone.

"What the hell is it?"

The sagging tits told me it was female. A jagged crown on its bald head told me it was royalty. The rest of it...from the jutting jowls and the craggy shark teeth, the soulless black bubble eyes on the sides of its head, and to the gill slits on the side of its thick neck screamed fish.

Underneath the portrait was one word: MOTHER.

I flipped through more pages and found other drawings of the same creature and all of them with the title MOTHER.

My family was 'A lineage to be treasured and honored.'

The sour rank fishy smell thickened. My throat felt tight.

"Pull over." I croaked. "Now."

Melinda pulled over to the side of the road. I stepped out and vomited into the weeds. I stood there, my hands on my knees and waited for my head to stop spinning.

I heard soft footsteps on the gravel as Melinda walked over to me and patted me on the back.

"Christ….are you trying to tell me that thing was Samuel's mother?"

"And his grandmother, and his great-grandmother, great-great grandmother ad nauseam."

"Jesus." I coughed spit out phlegm. "How did a nice girl like you get caught up with a fishguy like that?"

Melinda raised her fist and glared at me with such fury I was sure she was going to slug me.

"Don't call him that!" She growled low in her chest and stomped away.

"I'm sorry, truly."

She kicked the car's tire with enough force to shake the chassis.

"I didn't mean to upset you."

For the record, I have never meant those words more in my life.

"Forget it. My nerves are raw as hell…God, I need a cigarette." She smiled with tight lips and leaned against the car. "To answer your question, I inherited him. A friend of mine was helping him. Graham. One day I received a letter from Graham's lawyer. It was one of those "if you're reading this, I'm dead" sort of letters. Anyway, he wanted me to take over where he left off. Five years later and we're back to square one."

"What happened in Morley?"

"The official story was the Treasury department was taking down bootleggers and an unfortunate accident happened, a still exploded, and set the entire town on fire, killing hundreds."

"Why didn't this make the papers? I don't remember this."

"Sweetie, G-men make sure John Q. Public don't know any more than they need to know." Melinda shrugged. "From what I can gather, it was a joint coup. The military and a group of academics, if you can imagine such a partnership, an East coast Ivy League wannabe university. The villagers who weren't killed outright have been hunted down over the past ten years."

"What does the government want with them?"

Melinda's voice was soft and she halted between the words as if she were carefully dancing across stones in a rushing river. "Not all of our enemies live on the land. There are… things… out there, Jake, in the deep. The boys in the Ivory Towers are working with the military to make sure we throw the first punch, understand?"

"And Samuel….did he…"

"The raid interrupted the ritual. Not that he didn't get a good peek at what was passing as his 'bride'."

"I still can't get over the image. That *thing* is Samuel's…and he was expected to breed with it? It's unimaginable. Horrific."

"It's not important now. What is important is the fact Samuel is the last survivor. It makes him a rare commodity. Something your friends at the Odyssey Shop are desperate to sell to the Ivy League boys in the white coats."

"I told you they aren't my friends."

"So you keep saying." She looked at her wristwatch. "We need to get back on the road. I doubt Ricky will be able to keep those three boys at the coffee shop occupied much longer."

"Ricky?"

"An old friend. I slipped him some money to take them on a wild goose chase. It's the only reason we haven't been tailed."

"Clever."

"I've been doing this a long time but I'm almost out of tricks. Samuel is running out of time. I need to take him somewhere we can be safe."

We? A chill ran through me as we shared a look. For the first time, I noticed her eyes. They were caramel colored, kind but heavy and sad. "Melinda, are you and he…?"

She kicked the tire again.

"Oh, Melinda…don't tell me that you two…"

"I know I'm a damn fool but, hell, I love him. Samuel is the best and kindest man I have ever met and I don't want to lose him." She grabbed me by the shoulder, "And don't you dare tell Bear. If you think about spilling your guts to him, I'll take you down and this time I won't let you off so easy. You know I can, buster."

I held my hands up in submission. "My lips are zipped."

The sadness in her eyes grew heavier. "Do you know what breaks my heart? I don't know who I'll lose him to first. Those bastards who want to sell him to the highest bidder or to *her*. He says she still sings to him. Sometimes, the way he stares into the ocean...I don't know who he wants more. So, you see how crazy my life has been for the last five years? How impossible? Why I needed Bear's help to vanish? We're not just running from G-men and bounty hunters, Jake, we're trying to hide from the goddamn sea."

She took a deep breath. "God, I need a cigarette. It figures I'd be paired up with the only P.I that doesn't smoke. You ready?"

"As ready as I'll ever be. Where are we going?"

"How do you feel about clowns?"

CHAPTER SIX

A Lot of Things Happened Very Quickly

We passed by the tin sign of a grotesque laughing clown with bulging eyes who promised carnival goers FUN! FUN! FUN! at the Lake Pontcharttrain Amusement Park.

I never liked clowns. And I definitely wasn't in the mood for fun.

A few years ago, a man by the name of Batt built an amusement park on the shore of Lake Pontchartrain which isn't a lake; it is a salt water estuary that feeds into the Gulf of Mexico. In spite of hard times, people always found a few pennies stashed away to go have a whirl on the Ferris wheel, stroll down the boardwalk, or try their luck and knock over some tin monkeys to get a stuffed bear for a girl and, hopefully, a kiss.

Melinda parked the car in the empty parking lot.

"We walk from here. Samuel will be waiting for us on the beach."

"How will we find him?"

"How many other fishmen are you expecting to find?"

An elderly security guard was standing at the entrance. No words were said as Melinda gave him a smile and a few dollars. He tipped his hat, opened the gate and we were in like Flynn.

We walked straight through the park and made a beeline to the shore. Melinda wasn't wasting any time which was fine by me; there is nothing creepier than an amusement park after closing hours. The bright red, green and blue lights were turned off and we made our way by the light of the full moon. The air reeked of stale popcorn and the Ferris wheel creaked as the wind rocked the steel cages. All of the empty food stands and shooting galleries were closed for the night. Our footsteps crunching on the leftovers of the day were the only signs of life in the park.

The asphalt stopped at the edge of a fake sandy beach.

"There he is. Samuel!"

He didn't respond to her. I don't think he knew we were there. He had his back to us, a stout figure in a long coat, standing a little too much in the water for comfort's sake. His arms were raised high and his head was tilted backwards. I'm not a betting man but if I had to make a bet,

I would say Samuel was deep in prayer. To what, I knew in my gut I didn't want to know.

Melinda ran to him and I raced after her.

"Melinda...wait." I grabbed her by the arm and stopped her a few yards away from Samuel.

"What are you doing?" She tried to twist out of my grasp and screamed. "Let go!"

Samuel turned and....oh God...how to describe him?

In the moonlight, his skin was a translucent grayish green and it glistened as if he were sweating even though the air was chilly. His fedora rode low on his bald head and then I saw why. There were small, useless knobs where the outer ear used to be. I could see the hole flutter as if picking up sound on the air. His face was swollen and puffy. The skin drooped as if it were a rubber mask two sizes too big for his skull. His nose was flat and his lips were pinkish smears. But his eyes, good God. They were a milky blue, the color of a drowned man's eyes and jutted out of his head as if they were on the verge of popping out of the sockets. He sneered, revealing a row of sharp teeth. "Stay back!" he yelled, holding out a webbed claw.

Melinda stopped. "Why? What's wrong?"

Samuel cocked his head. He blinked lazily, a silver membrane slipped across from the sides of his eyes. "Can't you hear her? They are so close." His voice sounded clotty, like someone speaking through a thick gauze of phlegm. "She is coming for me."

"No! You can fight it. We can find somewhere to hide. Please, Samuel!"

"This is my choice." The soft skin around his throat jiggled as he struggled for breath. "My destiny."

"But....what about me? You're just going to leave me here?"

"Mel, sweetie, we were always fooling ourselves. It doesn't matter how much I love you. We can't be together."

"But can't we try? Find something that can reverse this? Make you back into the man you were?"

"That is what you have never understood, Melinda.. *This is what I am.*"

"But...."

Samuel opened his arms and she went to him for one long, last embrace.

I turned away, trying not to feel any more like a third wheel than I already did and saw three figures on the asphalt.

"STEP AWAY FROM THE SPECIMEN." A staticky voice screeched over a megaphone. "YOU HAVE UNTIL THE COUNT OF THREE."

"Oh, hell." The three trenchcoats from the coffee shop had found us. One held a megaphone. The other two held Tommy guns. One of those guns swerved right at me.

"ONE."

I held my hands high. "Melinda, do as the nice man says."

"TWO."

"Oh, for Chrissakes!" Melinda swore, pushed Samuel behind her, and pulled out a .38. "Can't a girl have one goddamn minute alone with her guy?!?"

I hit the sand. The trenchcoat covering me went down before the other one had a chance to pull his trigger.

"You bitch!" he said and a wave of bullets soared through the night at Melinda. I heard her scream as she collapsed.

Samuel ran at them, hissing and teeth snapping, fueled by frustration and fury at the sons of bitches who had hunted him down and shot his lady love.

It was a lovely gesture, truly. Sadly, bullets are not known for their appreciation of romantic overtures. He jerked like a marionette as the trenchcoat with the Tommy gun pumped him full of lead.

"NO!" I screamed as I wrestled with my own .38 and took pot shots at the trenchcoats. It was embarrassingly futile from my position, sitting on my ass in the sand, but my rage needed the release.

I fired the last bullet in the chamber and Tommy Gun Trenchcoat laughed. "You finished?"

I put my hands up. "Guess so."

He pointed the barrel at my face. I wondered how effective the Salt's curative powers were with massive traumatic head wounds.

I guess we were about to find out.

I tensed, waiting for the first volley of hot lead when Megaphone Man said, "What the hell?"

A low whistling howl from behind me answered him. I turned to see Samuel kneeling over Melinda, his head was thrown back and he blasted out a high pitched wail. I clasped my hands uselessly over my ears. There was no way to shield ourselves from the sound. It drilled through our skulls, wormed into our brains and shrieked down into our spinal cords like scalding quicksilver until me and the Trenchcoat Duo, were begging for the agony to stop.

Samuel belted out one more note and fell forward across Melinda's body.

In the numbing silence that followed, I lunged at Trenchcoat Tommy Gun, slamming my knee into his nuts and wrestled the gun from his hands.

Before I could congratulate myself for this burst of machismo, the Megaphone Man slid behind me and conked me on the head with his megaphone, opening a huge gash. I fell face first to the asphalt, blinking through the blood.

"Let go of the gun."

I released the gun and he kicked it away, taking some skin of my knuckles as he did it.

"If I had it my way, I'd splatter your precious brains all over this beach and leave you for the seagulls. So, keep still and don't give me a reason to have a happy accident, okay? George! Worry about your family jewels on your own time. Get up and go secure the specimen. I think it's dead."

George stood, groaned, and clutched his groin. He opened a duffel bag, pulling out some rope and a knife. "Bastard." he said after giving me a couple of vicious kicks in my gut.

Megaphone Man stood over me, one foot on my face, grinding my cheek across the rough gravel. "You son of a bitch. You couldn't leave well enough alone, could you? Thank Mama Effie for saving your sweet ass this time."

This time? My head reeled with those words. At what time had she ever saved any part of me much alone my ass?

He yelled over his shoulder. "Hey, how you coming, George? We've got a long drive and I can smell it from here."

"I'm working on it. He weighs a...what is ...Holy Mother of GOD!" George screamed. "What the hell is that? Coming out of the water...looks like dozens of...AH! Shit, he ain't dead! Christ! He's got me, Louis! Help! Help....oh my GOD...GOD! HEL-!"

"What the hell are you- UURGH!" he cried out as a hot river of blood gushed out onto me followed by two hundred pounds of Louis.

"Holy hell!" I screamed as I wriggled out from underneath the corpse. Once I was free, I followed a wet, munching sound that led to a *thing,* It was more like a frog than a fish, covered in grayish green algae flaked scales and squatted down on its haunches, busy making a grisly meal of what remained of Louis' heart.

"Oh shit."

My gun that Louis had kicked was a few feet away. I crabwalked to it, clumsily loaded the chamber, dropping bullets like breadcrumbs. Finally loaded, I slammed the cylinder shut and—

And then a lot of things happened quickly.

It stopped eating, stared dead straight at me, dropped the meaty lump, crouched down and, faster than I thought possible, jumped. My breath was knocked out of me as a hundred pounds of wet sand landed on my chest. I squeezed off a shot, purely by reflex, shooting into blind space. The monster slapped the gun out of my hand with a grunt and leered at me as hot, viscous drool dripped on my face through white, spiny teeth.

I sputtered and screamed as I tried to push the thing off me. Its flesh was impossibly squishy as if it had no bones. It hissed, releasing a blast of foul breath that smelled like hot, rotting fish soup. Fighting against the urge to vomit, I punched at its toothy maw and it engulfed my entire hand.

"Shit!" I tried to pull my hand out but the thing pulled back. It made a chortling noise, like thick laughter. *It was playing with me!* "You son of a…fish!"

The gun landed a foot out of my reach. I pulled and scrambled to get closer. The thing on me felt like a huge, wet blob and it wrestled with my arm, as if my pulling was part of the game. I scraped my fingers bloody against the asphalt until I reached the gun. "Yes!" I said in victory and slammed it under the bastard's jaw. I was about to squeeze the trigger and blow it to smithereens when I heard Samuel's gutteral voice scream out—

"Stop!"

Samuel ran to the monster and made a few high pitched clicks. The thing shook its head, like a naughty dog with a chewtoy.

"AAARGH, it's biting me! It burns! Get it off me or I swear I'll shoot it dead!"

Samuel slapped it in the head and hissed angrily at it until the thing released my hand, and scuttled away to the water. My hand was blistered and raw. Blood oozed from the bites.

Samuel helped me to my feet. "Sorry."

"A friend of yours?" I asked and put the gun back in my jacket pocket.

"A cousin or brother, more like."

The monster turned around, pulled my watch out of its kisser and dangled it before hopping off into the lake.

"That cocky son of a bitch."

Samuel's laughter was wet and globby. "They like shiny things. At least you still have a hand."

My hand was a mess but I could feel the Salt already working its magic. "You owe me a watch."

Samuel had taken off most of his clothes and I could see his chest was dotted with clotting holes. They were healing, right in front of my eyes.

"Nice trick there," I said, waving at his bullet holes.

"Family secret," Samuel said, shrugging.

"Wish I knew it." Melinda walked up from behind him, cradling her left arm "My chest hurts like a son of a bitch."

"Melinda! Thank God! How?"

"I told you, Jake, I've been doing this a long time." She tapped her chest and I heard a dull thud. "Brewster body shield. A waistcoast of eleven pounds of leather and steel scales. It'll stop a bullet but damn if you don't feel like you been hit by a truck. Too bad it didn't do much for my arm. It's all busted to hell."

"Well, you're in better shape than these guys," I said, pointing to the dead trenchcoats littering the beach. "Christ, we'd better get out of here before the cops come. Someone must've heard those gunshots."

"Let me do you one last favor."

Samuel let out a long, high pitched whistle followed by a series of clicks. A dozen of the weird frog fish monsters came hopping from behind him, answering in low pitched whistles and squeaks. The horrible smell of brine rolled off them, making me queasy. The one from before creeped over to me, hissing and unrolling a long tongue tasted the air around me. Samuel swatted it on the head and it snapped at Samuel before loping away to the others. They squabbled over the bodies, pulling and snatching pieces of bloody meat, reminding me of seagulls picking over trash left behind during low tide. A sweet, high whistle sounded and they all stopped fighting and dragged the bodies off into the water.

"Well, that does the trick."

"It is a long trip back home and they need to feed," Samuel said. "Now, I have a favor to ask of you." He put a scaly, webbed hand on my shoulder. I wish I can say it felt brotherly but, frankly, it gave me the creeps. "I need you to take care of Melinda."

"What? Excuse me? Hello? I'm standing right here." She butted herself inbetween us and lifted her chin in defiance. "What the hell do you think I am? Some kind of stray you need to find a new home for? You're just like every other man. You think I can't live on my own without big strong you?"

"Mel…" Samuel rubbed her cheek.

She slapped his hand away. "No. You don't get to touch me. I can take care of myself, thank you. I did perfectly fine before you barged into my life, Samuel Norcutt." Her lips quivered as she said his name and a tear slid stubbornly down her cheek. She wiped it away and gritted her teeth. "I can do fine without you. Do you hear me? So, just… go. Get out of here. No reason to keep *her* waiting."

That's when I noticed a tall, lithe figure approaching us coming from the lake. The swarm of frog things parted reverently out of its path. Unlike the others, it was dressed in a long, shimmering gown of dull white and pink. It reminded me of the underbelly of a salmon, the way it flashed in the moonlight. On its head it wore a crown of jagged spires as if someone had dipped a slice of coral reef in gold. Beneath the crown was the face I had seen drawn so many times in the Norcutt family journal. The bulbous, cold black eyes, the thick, grotesque turned up lips barely able to close over the rows and *rows* of thin, needle sharp teeth. It reached out its long, mottled arms and pointed at Melinda with its webbed claws.

"Mother, no!" Samuel hid Melinda behind himself. It hissed and knocked them both to the ground with a swipe of its clawed hand.

Mother slinked past them, ignoring them as it made a straightline to Yours Truly.

Inside my head, I heard singing, a song so crystal fine it took my breath away.

Hungry...I've traveled so far...must feed.

Its eyes locked onto mine and, holy Christ, I couldn't move, couldn't look away. The singing filled my soul. A soprano melody made my heartbeat slow down and my body feel like it was made of stone. I wanted to say something...to scream anything but I couldn't. My tongue felt like a dead root in my mouth.

It stood close to me, its long, webbed claws on my shoulders, holding me tight. Its eyes were as big as saucers, round and black but dotted with silver spots of light mesmerizing me. Its skin was was a rainbow of scales twinkling in the moonlight. The air shimmered and it transformed into a beautiful woman, long blonde hair and...my gaze shifted downwards....a body a goddess would wage a war to possess. Her hands, creamy white with long delicate fingers, ran through my hair and I felt a deep sense of calm and, sweet Jesus...desire. Her siren song made my blood rush and I wanted this woman with every fiber of my being. I pulled her to me and kissed her, hard, our tongues tasting each other and then, suddenly…she pushed me away and grimaced as if she had bitten into something rotten. She shook her head as if trying to get rid of a bad taste.

You are tainted. Poisoned!

I'm not going to lie; it hurt my feelings. But at least whatever hold it had over me was broken. The glamour covering it fell away like whitewash and it was revealed as the horrible fish thing I had seen in the journals. I could now move and I did. My hand went straight to the gun in my pocket. I pulled it out, cocked back the hammer and pointed it straight at its head.

It opened its maw, showing me every row of spiny teeth as it howled at my impertinence.

Samuel ran to me. "No, Jake! Don't."

"Why not? If I kill it, you can be free."

"You can't kill her, Jake, all you can do is hurt her and if you do, all of the others, the ones out there in the deep… and there are hundreds of them, Jake…. will swarm this beach. They won't waste a second in killing you and Melinda. I won't be able to stop them."

"But...it's not fair. What was the point of all of this if we can't save you? If you two can't find somewhere to run to?"

"*THIS* is what I am, Jake, for better or worse. *They* are my family and out there, with them, is where I belong."

"It's true, Jake." Melinda hugged her bleeding, broken arm close to her chest. "None of this is fair but it is what needs to be done. Sometimes, the guy doesn't get the girl." She kissed Samuel on the cheek. "Go. Go, now. Before I change my mind."

CHAPTER SEVEN

My Silent Partner, Revived

"...but family is family, I guess."

Giovanna sits and silently listens as I ramble on and on, trying to sort things out by talking to her.

"Melinda and I watched Samuel walk off into the lake. We stayed for a bit, not saying anything, just waiting, I guess, for some sort of sign. Then a pair of pants rolled onto the shore. I guess he wasn't going to need modesty where he was going.

"I offered to drive Melinda to the hospital but she refused. She said she knew a guy who wouldn't ask any questions. He did a bang up job setting Melinda's arm. I let him bandage my hand for appearances sake. He had quite a setup down in the embalming room of his funeral home. I guess fixing living bodies isn't too different than fixing dead ones, in the long run.

"She brought me home which was a godsend since I don't think I could've paid a cabbie to drive me. Not in this state." I sit back and stare at my long suffering audience. My blood is staining her face with a pink smear, like the blush of a young girl.

"Well, that's it for tonight. Or this morning. Whatever time it is. Thanks for listening, Giovanna. What would I do without you?"

I walk to the fire escape ladder and from behind me I hear, "Jake Is…Isten..?"

My shoulders slump. I am too tired for this.

"ISH-ten-HEDGY. Seriously, it's not that hard." I turn and I am blinded by a bright light flashed in my face. I hold up my hand to shield my eyes. I can make out two figures, men, I think, from the fedoras and long coats.

"It's him," the voice behind the light says. "Pacu, tag him."

A shorter figure moves out from behind him, holds up a long stick, and I hear a PFFFT, PFFT sound.

I feel the darts as they slam into my chest. I have barely enough time to utter, "What the?" before I feel the warm rush of the drugs flood my veins. My hand fumbles as I try to pull out my gun. My fingers are like sausages, fat and engorged, and the gun tumbles from my hand. As I fall, it slides across the floor.

My chest heaves as I struggle to draw in breath. I am completely conscious though completely paralyzed. Three men are standing over me. *Who are these bastards?*

The short one is dark skinned with tattoos on his face. He grimaces and I notice his teeth are filed into points. "Gods, he's a mess."

"Put on your gloves, gentlemen." A tall man with round spectacles says. "We don't know what is contaminated and what is not."

The third is built like a bulldog, squat and all muscle. "It's going to be a long ride to—"

The sound of my gun firing rips through the air and three men fall dead around me like sheaths of wheat.

I hear soft footsteps. I can't see who is coming and my heart beats faster, pushing the poison through my system. I try to speak but all I can break through my frozen lips is the "W" sound of "Who?"

A beautiful woman with long, black hair and dark eyes as sharp and fierce as a hawk leans over and kisses me. She takes a deep breath as if it is the sweetest thing she has ever tasted and smiles.

"Hello, Jake." She kisses me again. "What *would* you do without me?"

Giovanna?

The End

JAKE ISTENHEGYI:

THE ACCIDENTAL DETECTIVE

Road Trips, Acid Baths and One-Eyed Bastards

For my son, Daniel, who asked a very pointed question: "What did she do with his heart?"

CHAPTER ONE

The Year of Jake

I feel pretty good.

Even though I had just driven three solid days from New Mexico and my ass is as flat as a board.

Even though Mama Effie glares at me while I pull up in front of the Odyssey Shop in a car that is definitely not the one she loaned me.

Even though I lost the girl, had my head turned into tomato paste, and still have no gold in my pockets, I feel pretty damn good.

Because beside me I have a box that holds something better than gold.

I step out of the car, stretch, and take a deep breath. A brand-new year is only four days away and I really think this is going to be my year. The Year of Jake. I can feel it.

"Excuse me, bud." A man comes up to me, smiling. "Are you Jake Istenhegyi?"

"Yes, I am. Good morning!" I say before I notice the gun in his hand.

Because of course there is.

Secret Weapon

It was a weird night.

I'm not the kind of guy that is often hogtied on my patio with a beautiful woman kissing me on the lips.

I've never been that lucky.

Six hours ago, I was fighting for my life on a fake beach against very real sea monsters.

Two hours ago, I was regaling a cold statue on my patio about aforesaid nightmarish adventure.

An hour ago, I was accosted by three men who asked me my name, shot me with tranquilizer darts and tied me up.

They were then shot down by the aforementioned beautiful woman who is currently kissing me.

I tried speaking with a tongue that felt like a flap of leather and mumbled out, "Geeobanna?"

She ruffled my hair. "You're so cute when you're drunk."

In my defense, she was a marble statue in my garden only minutes before.

The patio door slammed open as Mama Effie came roaring through. "YOU STUPID BOY! What in the name of all that is holy did you-" She stopped midsentence as she noticed the three dead men littering the ground. "What mess is this now?"

I tried to unwrap myself from the ropes but ended up getting more entangled. "Wait a minnit. I can ecksplain."

"OH, can you?" Mama Effie hugged herself with her spidery arms. Despite the early hour, she had time to fix her hair, do her makeup and put on a dark coat lined with fox fur on the collar. She was dressed to kill. I just hoped it wasn't me.

"Why don't you start by introducing me to this sweet piece of pie you got fondling your roped-up unmentionables?"

Giovanna stood and faced Mama Effie. "I am Contessa Giovanna Lucia Lombardi-Bonham." She held my .38 on Mama Effie. "And, for your information, I'm responsible for this mess, not Jake."

"Oh, is that so?" She moved towards Giovanna until the muzzle pressed against her chest. "Let me introduce myself. I am Mama Effie, and, for your information, I run things here. Do you plan on making more mess on my patio?"

Mama Effie glared down into her rival's face. Giovanna's fingers tensed on the trigger. The temperature dropped ten degrees as they stared into each other's eyes.

Giovanna flipped the gun around and held the grip out to Mama Effie. "No. I think I've done enough damage."

"Smart girl. I might get to like you despite the company you keep." She took the gun and slipped it into her pocket. "Did you know any of these poor bastards?

"Not personally," said Giovanna. "But I know who they work for. More will be coming and very soon."

"Good to know. You finish unwrapping Houdini, take him upstairs to his apartment and sober him up. I'll call my cleanup crew."

Giovanna was remarkably strong. She stood about 5'6'' in her bare feet, weighed 130 pounds if she ate a big meal and was dressed in a gossamer dressing gown. She looked like a fairy tale princess, but brother, she had the grip of a mountain gorilla. I couldn't have resisted if I wanted to. She dragged me up a flight of stairs and into my apartment.

"How are you feeling?"

"Like I'm made of rubber."

"Get out of those clothes and into a hot shower. Hurry! We don't have much time."

"Why? Who is coming?"

"It's a long story. I'll tell you when we get on the road."

I slumped on the edge of my bed battled my shoes with my fat sausage fingers.

"Good grief, let me do that."

"Hey! I can do it!"

She slapped my hands away and pulled off my shoes. "What are you afraid of? I'll see something I haven't seen before? God, men never change." She unbuckled my belt, pulled off my pants, yanked my shirt over my head and in a blink of an eye I was naked.

"Now, get going!" She pulled me to my feet and pushed me towards the bathroom. "Lucio will already have men on the road by now."

"Who?"

"Lucio Amara. Do yourself a favor and scratch that name into your brain."

"Why?"

"Because he's the man coming to get you." She turned on the water, full stream. "But don't worry; you have a secret weapon. *Me*. Get in!"

"Christ! It's boiling!"

"The heat will help metabolize the drugs faster. We need to get on the road within the hour."

"Where are we going?"

"Somewhere safe."

CHAPTER THREE

Road Trip

I stepped out of the bathroom with a towel wrapped around my waist to find Mama Effie sitting on my bed, tapping her foot impatiently.

"Jesus, does privacy mean anything to anyone around here?"

"We need to talk, Boy, about where you were earlier this evening."

"I was at Lake Pontchartrain, fighting sea monsters, as one does."

"Don't get smart with me. I need answers."

"To what? You haven't asked any questions."

"The two men who were following you. Where are they?"

"There were three, actually. And I thought your bosses sent them to follow Melinda Page and Samuel not me."

"Six of one, half a dozen of the other." Mama Effie rolled her eyes. "They are missing and I'm on the hook. What happened to them?"

"It's a long story."

"Give me the highlights."

I went to my closet, pulled out a pale blue dress shirt, a pair of black twill pants and started to dress. I tried to figure out the best way to highlight the nightmare that happened without sounding like a lunatic. In the end, it was just easier to tell it how it happened.

"One of them, I didn't get his name, Melinda Page shot dead. Pow. Right between the eyes. The two others, George and Louis, I think were their names, were killed by fishmen who swam in via the ocean inlet."

I selected a tie, dark blue with burgundy checks, and wrapped it around my collar. "You won't find their bodies so don't bother looking. They were dragged off. Snacks for the road, Samuel said."

"And where are Samuel and Melinda?"

"Melinda dropped me off and left for parts unknown. If you want to find Samuel, how long can you hold your breath?"

"Samuel has gone deep, then? The Bosses won't like that." Mama Effie arched her brow as she tapped her rouged cheek "Ah, well, *c'est la vie*."

"That's it?" It was my turn to raise an eyebrow. "You lose your prize catch and hear that Fishmen from the Deep Blue Sea eat your goons and all you can say is, '*C'est la vie*'?"

"They weren't my boys, or it would be a different matter but I'll let their handlers know," she said as she went to the door. "Are you finished preening? Your lady friend downstairs isn't the patient sort."

"I'll be there soon. I have to check on something first."

After she left, I went down to Bear's office. The room was worse than empty. It was hollow. Not even a whiff of his horrible aftershave in the air.

"Damn."

Bear was still 'on sabbatical' or whatever ghosts did when they ran low on juice. The last time I saw my friend, he looked as wispy as cheesecloth. I was afraid he would never come back.

I grabbed one of his beloved *Black Mask* magazines, just in case I needed him. It was a ghost trick we learned recently. Normally, if he tries to leave the confines of the Odyssey Shop, he pops back into his office, but, for some weird reason, where a *Black Mask* went, so did Bear.

I rolled up the magazine and slid it inside my jacket pocket and closed the door behind me.

"What's the hold up?" Giovanna called from downstairs.

"On my way."

She was waiting for me at the bottom of the stairs.

"That's a new look," I said.

Giovanna had taken liberties of my closet while I was showering and dressed in a pair of khaki pants that she belted tightly around her waist and a white dress shirt with rolled up sleeves. She found a pair of black and white saddle shoes from somewhere in the store. Her long, raven hair was cut into a short tomboy bob. She looked like a waif in a Chaplin film.

"New life, new look. Every thirty years or so is the best rule of thumb. It's something you'll need to think about as the years roll by."

"I didn't know there was a rulebook."

"Don't worry. I'll show you the ropes. Ready to hit the road? Mama Effie is loaning us a car and I've already loaded it with essentials. Don't worry about clothes; we'll pick up what we need on the way."

"On whose dime?"

"Mine. I'm very wealthy, you know."

"Oh, really?"

"Of course. Who wants to spend immortality a pauper?"

"Another trick I hope you teach me. So, where are we going?"

"I'll drive. But, first, where are we exactly?"

I took her by the hand. "I'll do the driving. You just tell me where to point the car."

CHAPTER FOUR

Company's Here

A car waited for us in the alley behind the Odyssey Shop. It was a beautiful Phaeton sedan, two toned, silver and black. It made me long for my car that was destroyed in Harleaux's barn when it burned down. The Phaeton was parked behind a white van with the logo 'Sunshine Butchers on the side. Two men in blue overalls slung a child sized body bag into the back. Mama Effie gave a thick white envelope to the driver of the van before he drove off.

"Remind me not to ask what you put in your jambalaya."

"This is the second mess you've gotten me into in less than 24 hours. You owe me." She snapped her fingers and a goon scrambled over to her side. "I'll be collecting the minute you come back. Keep that in mind."

I opened the car door for Giovanna, she slid in and pulled out a road map.

"And take care of my car," Mama Effie said. "If there is one scratch on it, I swear, I'll take it out of your lily-white hide."

"Just add it to my tab."

"Oh, I will. And I want it returned with a full tank of gas."

I got in behind the wheel. Leather bench seat, plush and comfortable. The dashboard looked marbleized and matched the steering wheel. Oh, yes. This had Mama Effie's style all over it. I started the ignition. The engine purred like a satiated lion.

In the backseat were two boxes full of food and jugs of water. Next to them was a tarp-covered crate. I reached over the seat and pulled back the tan oilskin. I saw guns and bullets. Lots of guns and bullets.

"What sort of party are you expecting?"

"A dangerous one." She pulled a switchblade knife from her pants pocket and tried the trigger. The silver blade popped out with a metallic ching.

Mama Effie tapped on the passenger window.

"Two weeks?"

Giovanna pursed her lips. "Maximum. If longer than that...," she shrugged. "I don't think it will matter much. We'll probably be dead."

"Wait? Who'll be dead?"

"Shush, Boy, grownups are talking." Mama Effie patted Giovanna's shoulder. "You take care. If you need anything, call. I'll pull out all the stops."

"Will do."

"And for the record," Mama Effie said as she pushed away, "my jambalaya is excellent."

"I'll be the judge of that," I said and put the car into gear. I drove a few feet down the alley when a jet-black Packard pulled up and blocked my path. Four men popped out of the Packard and started firing tommy guns.

"Go! Go! Go!" Giovanna screamed.

"Where!?"

"THROUGH!"

I slammed my foot on the gas, skimmed between the car and the side of the road, balancing on two wheels as we drove through a storm of bullets. The reinforced windshield cracked but held.

In the rearview mirror, I could see Mama Effie's goons circle around her and get her to safety while two others stayed to guard the rear. I saw the bodyguard's flinch as the bullets crashed into their chests.

"Are you hurt?" I turned to look at Giovanna.

"Don't worry about me, Handsome." Her face was flushed with excitement and her eyes sparkled. She rolled down the window, leaned out and fired six bullets into the crowd. Three men went down. "Yes!" she screamed as she slid back into her seat and reloaded.

Ahead of us, another Packard came at us, fast.

"Giovanna, we have company."

"*Merda*! How did he get here so damn fast?" She slid down to the floorboard and slammed more bullets into the chambers.

A sparkle of sunlight on metal from the car caught my attention. In the backseat was a man with a silver eyepatch. It was only for a flash, a millisecond of time, but in that moment, I knew he was looking straight at me.

Stop the car.

A sharp tingle stabbed my fingertips. It was a *pulling*, like magnets attracted to one another. I felt it before when I touched the crystal sphere in the Cross of Trismegitus that held a sliver of Salt.

STOP THE CAR. NOW.

A cloud descended over my head, like a drunk giving into sleep. I felt a strange tug and my foot eased off the gas.

"Jake! *Dammit!*"

I heard a CHING and felt a searing pain as Giovanna slammed her switchblade into my shin.

"What the hell?!?"

"Just getting your attention. Now, drive!"

I pounded my foot hard on the gas. The tires squealed spraying rocks and grass as we got the hell away from whatever was in that Packard.

CHAPTER FIVE

Family Issues

"How's your leg?"

"It'll heal. I've had worse."

Giovanna crawled out from the floorboard, rested her chin on her knees and looked over at me with wide, almond eyes. With her pageboy haircut, she looked like an orphaned waif, innocent and harmless. But it was just a cover. Contessa Giovanna Lucia Lombardi-Bonham was a survivor and, if pushed into a corner, a dangerous predator. It's amazing what you learn about a person when a road trip begins with a shower of bullets.

"So, where are we going?" I asked.

"West, to New Mexico."

"That's a change of scenery."

"Archibald loved the desert; he had asthma. I have a laboratory there. We did some of our best work there." She smiled but her eyes were misty. "It's a good place to hide."

"I thought you'd want to go back to your house in Illinois." I remembered where I first laid eyes on her. It was a fairy tale palace tucked away in the wooded area of Central Illinois, full of expensive antiques and art. On the mantle above the fireplace were framed pictures chronicling her life with her husband, Archibald and son, Arthur. I found her beside the pool, green ivy already curling around her cold, marble arms.

Giovanna shook her head and stared coldly at the road. "Always lead your enemy."

"Okay, New Mexico, then. It's going to be a long ride but, luckily, we've got plenty to talk about. So, tell me about Lucio Amara."

"The best thing I can say is that I'd like him better if he'd stayed dead the first time I killed him."

"Okay, you're going to have to lengthen that story."

She took a deep breath. "The year was 1455 and my father and I had finally found the elixir to immortality."

"Wait, how old are you?"

She pinned me with a stare.

"Sorry, continue."

"My father was an alchemist. As soon as I could be trusted to hold a beaker steady, I was his assistant. The laboratory was my playground. I cut my teeth on Latin and Greek. After that, he introduced me to all the mathematics and science that were available at the time. He didn't care that I was a girl. He was happy to have someone he could confide in.

"The earlier formulas of the elixir were tested on rats, rabbits, whatever was handy. Finally, we had our first success. A rat called Rattio."

"Rattio?"

"Pia named it. She was always naming the animals and giving them fancy funerals when they died. Everything was a party for that girl."

"How many other animals did you have like that?"

"No others. Father didn't want to waste time, so we progressed to human trials."

"Where would he get the people?"

"Father had his ways. In those days, when you needed a person cured or killed, you called an alchemist. My father knew secrets that could've toppled noble families and many powerful men owed him favors. It was nothing for him to obtain prisoners that had been sentenced to death. Father would get them, five at a time. We kept them in cages in the laboratory."

"And Lucio?"

"He was a dirty, thief that had the misfortune of picking the wrong pocket. There wasn't anything special about him if that's what you're asking. It was the luck of the draw that he survived."

"The Salt was dangerous?"

"No, not the elixir. It was the test afterward. When we cut out his heart."

"Oh." I thumbed my breastbone remembering how Harleaux had carved out my heart for an arcane ritual to trap me inside her shrunken skull prison.

"Don't look so serious. His grew back. Obviously."

"Thankfully. So, what happened?"

"There was a fire in the lab. My father was killed. I saved the elixir and as many notes as I could carry. My sisters and I fled and kept running."

"From who?"

"The Order of Zosimos. Twelve of the wealthiest bankers in the Republic of Florence. We weren't the only ones looking for immortality. There were many other alchemists with rich patrons, all of them scrabbling over lost books, occult trinkets, anything to curry favor to keep the money flowing into their pockets.

"Somehow, after the fire, Lucio was taken into their cabal and they found a way to create a seed crystal from his blood.

"And they were the ones that burned down his lab and killed your father?"

She shrugged.

"And they are still after you? How many?"

She sighed and looked out the window at the scenery that rolled past. "All I know is that the Order started with twelve plus Lucio. I don't know their entire roster, but I know that four of the original twelve are alive, in some sense of the word. But as for Lucio, I have no doubt that son of a bitch is still around."

"Why?"

"He sends me postcards."

I let that sink in.

"So, what does he want with me?"

"Lucio's blood has been the source of the Order's elixir for 500 years. After all this time, the potency must be getting thin. From what I hear, most of the oldest members live in a twilight sleep. Alive, but not cognizant. Lucio is tapped out. They need a new well to draw from and because you took an entire dose of the new, more powerful Elixir that I created, you are the purest source of the Salt in the world."

"Am I looking a gift horse in the mouth? Maybe I could make a quick buck if they want me so badly."

"Jake, if they find you, they will strap you to a board, jam needles into your veins, milk you, bring you to the point of death and wait until you recover before they start the process over and over again until they have a workable crystal synthesized from the Salt in your blood."

"Damn. That's terribly descriptive. How do you know?"

"I know because it's what I would've done, once upon a time."

*****

It was dark by the time we reached Dallas. The blinking lights of the Oleander Court Motel beckoned me like a siren, and I parked in the first open stall. The building was an ugly, squatting box made from sun-bleached stucco and topped with a faded red tiled roof. Attached to it was a meat and three restaurant called Delilah's Diner that boasted the best chicken fried steak in Dallas. I didn't know how steak could be chicken fried but, at this point, I didn't care. The only food we'd had since New Orleans were some Necco wafers from a gas station and right now I'd eat the damn cow raw.

I got out of the car and needles ran down my thighs as blood rushed through my numbed legs. Giovanna got out and stretched her long, slender arms, waved her fingers to the sky, and bent from the waist, saluting the world in a whole different way. I felt my blood rush back up into more familiar areas.

We got a room under the names of Mr. and Mrs. Robertson. The bored teenage girl at the desk didn't ask any questions and we didn't offer any answers.

We made a beeline towards Delilah's Diner. It was a square looking building much like the motel except the stucco was painted pink. It was a dingy place, yellow orange curtains that did nothing to hide the newspapers taped to the cracked windows. There were three square tables, five chairs and stained paper menus. The waitress that took our order had a hump like a camel and all the grace of the same. She brought out our food, grunted and shuffled back to the kitchen.

"*Bon appetit,*" I said as I cut into the hunk of meat that defined itself as chicken fried steak. What lay on my plate looked to my eyes like a gastric nightmare but my stomach wasn't as critical. It tasted surprisingly good, despite the gristle.

Giovanna didn't seem to harbor my reservations and tore into the meal with gusto.

"It's funny. I just realized that you don't have much of a resemblance to either one of your sisters. They were blonde and so fair."

"I'm like a crow in a flock of snowy doves, is that what you're implying?"

"No...no, nothing like that. It just struck me how different you are from them."

"Pia and Piera's mother was a straw haired chambermaid that slept her way up the domestic ladder by marrying my father. She died popping out a pair of twins for her trouble. My mother, on the other hand, was the esteemed Dama Antinori Lombardi, of the house of Accardo, youngest daughter of Baron Amerigo Accardo."

"So, are you telling me that I'm sitting in the presence of royalty?"

"Barely. And royalty isn't such a cushy life. A daughter was fortuitous only as a bill of sale in those days. Her father used her virginity to settle an apothecary bill with my father."

"And I thought I had family issues."

"Darling, after five hundred years, I own an entire library."

We ate the rest of the meal in silence. I was thankful for the peace. My head was too tired to think about all that had happened or ponder on the vague threats waiting in New Mexico. The lump of meat turned into coal in my stomach at the thought.

Christ, Janos....you really stepped in it this time.

"Pia was right," Giovanna blurted out, her mushy voice breaking into my fugue. Her mouth was full of some kind of sticky bun mess they served as dessert. "That girl was an idiot, but she was right about one thing."

"What's that?"

"Life." She held up her syrupy fingers and grinned. "It's supposed to be messy."

"You can say that again."

"And I wasted so much time being the solid one, the smart one. But not this time. No, sir. Life is just a buffet of pleasures and, buster, this time I'm going to eat them all."

She reached out and stroked the back of my hand.

"So, what do you say, *Mr. Robertson*? Want to help me with the first course?"

That feeling of warmth spread back into my veins as I looked into her eager, dark brown eyes. Excitement rushed over me and I said, "Check, please!"

CHAPTER SIX

A Means to an End

There was no love; lust, yes, but I'd never delude myself into thinking it was anything romantic. I was a means to an end, a warm blanket of flesh that kept her from whatever harsh reality she was hiding from. I could settle for that except when I heard her sobbing when she thought I was asleep. I'd feel the sheets rustle as she turned to me, pull me close and hide her face in my chest, as if I couldn't feel the wetness of her cheek against my skin. It broke my heart and made me feel sick inside. I wanted to ask her what scared her so much, what made her tremble and turned her skin turn so white with dread...but I knew she'd smile that sly tigress smile, cover my lips with hers and it would end up in another rumble in the bedsheets.

Not that I'm complaining.

CHAPTER SEVEN

A Quick Phone Call Home

The sun was barely over the horizon when I slipped away from Giovanna.

The cool air made my skin prickle as I walked across the parking lot to the only payphone in sight.

"Operator."

"Get me 555-Delta. Ask for Mama Effie," I said. "Oh, and reverse the charges."

She was going to hate me for that.

A few clicks later and the melodious voice answered, "I'm going to add this to your tab."

"I assumed nothing less. Any news?"

"On the bozos that shot up my backyard and tried to kill me? Don't worry about them. It's sorted. My boys did find something odd in a pouch around the little one's neck."

"What? Identification?"

"Nothing so pedestrian. He had a small glass vial with what looks like a piece of meat inside."

"Are they pulling your leg?"

"Nobody pulls my leg. I have it right here. And here's something ever weirder: it's throbbing. Any idea what this could be?"

"Not a clue."

"By the way, do you know Raymond Bishop?"

"No. Who's he?"

"A very inquisitive private investigator from Los Angeles who is making a lot of waves looking for you. I thought maybe you had a new friend to play detective with."

"Did he leave a message?"

"I'm not your goddamn secretary."

"Ok, I'll deal with him when we get back."

"Oh, and one more thing. Didn't there used to be a statue on the patio?"

CHAPTER EIGHT

A Stranger on the Road

The worst thing about Texas is there's too goddamn much of it.

We left Dallas and drove for what felt like a week even though Giovanna assured me we had been on the road for only three hours. I don't know why she would lie but the endless brown and tan visas rolling past made me question her judgement. The deadness of the Southwest in winter leaves me to wonder if this was what the moon looked like. The only movements were stray tumbleweeds stumbling across the road.

Still, I couldn't ask for a more charming traveling companion. Giovanna took on the mantle of hostess and did her best to entertain me. She opened her entire life to me, telling stories about her adventures.

"I met William Shakespeare once. Traveling through London, I was invited to a dinner party where I was, quite accidentally, seated beside him. He gave me a pass to see a play."

"That's amazing. Which one?"

"I don't remember. I didn't go."

"What?!"

"He was just a dirty actor with bad teeth to me. The thing I remember most about him was how much he drank. Oh, and his breath. He could kill a cow at ten paces. I gave my ticket to my friend who adored all that silliness. A year later, I heard they became lovers and Shakespeare wrote some poetry for him." She laughed. "I missed out on being a part of literary history!"

The only time her voice lost its sparkle was when she spoke about her husband and son.

"We met in Belize. We were both searching for the Emperor's Blazing Tongue, a rare orchid that was thought to be extinct. Archibald wanted to save a sample to grow in his greenhouse. I wanted to grab as many of the little buggers I could find to crush into a new elixir. Our first meeting wasn't very favorable.

"We were married for five years when we decided to try and have a child. It wasn't easy. I had fourteen miscarriages. My body saw the fetus as a tumor and absorbed it. It's the elixir at work, you see, constantly repairing our bodies. But we were determined to work around it. There had to be a way and my husband...my Archibald...he was a genius. Together, we made a miracle. My boy, Arthur." Her lips smiled at his name, but her eyes stayed sad. "The next twenty years that I lived with my two boys were the most alive I ever felt. Arthur died in the war and Archibald faded away a few years later. Without them, what did life have to offer me? That's why I decided not to take the infusion of Salt and sent it to Bear to give to my sisters. I had hoped to die, to join my boys in whatever lies outside this world. Fat good it did me. They are lost to me." She turned her face as she tried to hide wiping a tear from her eye. "But enough about me. Tell me about you."

"Me?"

"Yes, you. Tell me, who is Jake Istenhegyi?"

"Considering how I talked your ear off when you were in my patio, I figure you'd know me better than anyone. You could hear me, right? Back when you were a...you know."

"A marble doorstop? Yes. It's like being in a small dark box with just my thoughts. I would've gone insane if you hadn't rescued--"

"Stole."

"Call it what you will. You took me home, planted beautiful flowers around me and talked to me. It made my hell a little more comfortable. And I see what you did there, clever boy. Trying to distract me. Now, tell me about you."

I clenched the steering wheel. The leather twisted under my grip as I struggled to think of anything to say.

"There's not much to say. Not really. Spent most of my life in boarding schools, all over Europe. England, Italy, Germany. My family is in Budapest but I'm not welcomed back home."

"Why not? You don't strike me as a black sheep."

"More like a stain on the good Istenhegyi name."

"What in the world did you do?"

"Be born. I am the evidence of an illicit affair dear old dad had with a beautiful Gypsy girl."

"Romantic."

"You think so? My father said she left me when I got sick as a baby. She tried to cure me by burning circles on my neck."

"Ah. Cupping. They still do that?"

"I guess so. I had scars but the Salt took care of that."

"And she left you? That doesn't sound right. I suspect there is more to that story that your father didn't tell you."

"I wouldn't be surprised. He's never been a very forthright guy. I had a picture of her, but it was stolen." Acid boiled in my stomach as I remembered all I had lost that night when Harleaux left me to flounder in the swamp. My mother's photo, her letter and the amulet she made me. She sent them to me via my half-brother, Radu, who then stole a fortune in gold from me and ran off to parts unknown. The bastard.

"So, why did want to be a private investigator?"

"I didn't. Like most things in my life, I fell into it.

"I was a twenty-year-old kid with no goals, dumped in New Orleans with orders from my father to take over my Uncle Andor's shop. No clue as to what I was supposed to do when I got there.

"And then I met Bear.

"He rented office space in the Odyssey Shop for Barrington Gunn Investigations. Sometimes he didn't have the cash for the rent so, in lieu of payment, he offered to take me as an apprentice. I'm not really a detective. My friend, Bear, was the one with dreams of being Sam Spade."

"So, why did you do it?"

"I was bored." I laughed, realizing the hard truth of the matter. "It was all harmless fun until it all went to hell. If I only knew then what I know now."

"What do you mean?"

"I mean, if I never started playing Watson to his Holmes, I wouldn't be on the run from a 500-year-old immortal alchemist. I would never have had zombie chickens peck at my legs, see a Boodaddy possessed corpse rip a man from limb to limb or wrestle with an inbred fishman. And, ten to one, I'd be happier for it."

Giovanna looked wistfully out the window. "True. But Bear would have been left unavenged, Melinda and Samuel would've been captured by God knows who and I'd still be sitting poolside, getting shit on by birds. It's selfish but, I'm glad you're a part of this crazy world, Jake Istenhegyi. I owe you and... what's that? Ahead of us on the side of the road?"

There was a tall dark shape creeping slowly, bobbing slightly like a drunk black swan. As we got closer, details became clearer. It was a steamer trunk, hoisted long side up, and someone was on the underside, carrying it.

"What the hell?"

As we passed by, I slowed down to a crawl get a good look at who was bearing the weight of Atlas on his shoulders.

The unfortunate stopped in his tracks, looked over, and saw me.

My foot slammed on the brake and we screeched to a stop. I pulled the car to the side of the road, yanked the brake and turned off the engine.

"What is it?" said Giovanna. "Jake! We don't have time for this!"

"We're going to make time. That's the son of a bitch who stole my gold!"

*****

"Oh, shit!" Radu, my thieving, half-brother shouted. He dropped the trunk and started running into the dead lands.

He was a few steps ahead of me but my red-hot anger gave me an edge. I tackled him and he instantly rolled up in a ball, covering his face and balls.

I pulled him over and yanked his hands away from his face. One eye was nearly fused shut. The right side of his jaw was a black-blue bruise.

"Don't!" he yelled. "Not the face!"

"Where is my gold, Radu?"

"I got jumped, okay? They took everything except that trunk. That's all I got on me."

"You stupid son of...aaargh!" I shouted and got off him. I kicked the ground, sending up clods of red dirt and screamed in frustration. "You lost all my gold? I'm going to kill you."

"Stop! Wait!" he said, snuffling. "I sent most of the gold ahead to Los Angles. General delivery."

I turned towards him. "What did you say?"

"It's in a box, at the main post office in Los Angles. The gold is waiting for us...." The poor sap smiled lopsidedly. "Brother."

"Jake." Giovanna walked up behind me, holding her stomach. "Who is this man?"

"This piece of shit is my half-brother, Radu."

"My name is Jake now," he said.

"No, it's not!" I said, kicking at him. "That's not your real name."

"It's not your real name either, *Janos*."

"Shut up, you dirty, gypsy, THIEF! You're lucky I don't just shoot you right here!"

"Stop it! Both of you." Giovanna stepped in between us. "Men. You never change."

"HE stole my gold!"

"It was a loan! I was going to pay you back when I hit it big in Hollywood."

"Christ, spare me your delusions of grandeur."

"And I told you, most of it is in Los Angles."

"Fine. Get up. We're going to Los Angeles."

"No, Jake," she insisted. "We need to get to my lab in New Mexico."

"Why? One place is as good as the other to hide out."

"Because." She turned away from Radu and pulled up her shirt. Her stomach was flaked with grayish scales, mottled dark spots of calcified flesh. She was turning into stone, right before my eyes.

"Jesus, Giovanna, when did this happen?"

"This morning. I don't how much time I have left but I don't want to waste it judging a pissing contest between you two so, let's get moving!"

Homecoming

Radu's whining in the backseat was making the snubnose .38 in my pants pocket heavier with each mile.

"I don't understand why we couldn't strap my trunk onto the roof, that's all I'm saying."

"You're lucky I didn't strap you onto the roof, so shut up."

"Boys, please."

Radu glared at me from the backseat, squished between the door and the boxes of ammo and food, and stared out the window to sulk.

Giovanna was quiet and pale.

"How are you doing?"

She replied with a weak smile.

"What can I do?"

"Just get me to my lab. Quickly."

I pushed the gas pedal to the floor. Texas flew past like a bad dream and we crossed into New Mexico by noon, sailed through some of the most desolate land I had ever seen and pulled up to her gate by three o'clock.

The house behind the gate was a complete flip from the European style villa from where I found Giovanna in

Illinois. It was a one story, Spanish adobe style building with a flat Mission Revival styled roof, tiles of sunburnt clay, pinkish white walls with wooden dowels jutting out every foot and circular windows. It butted up against a hillside dotted with scrub grass until the two were indistinguishable.

"Archibald's design?" I asked.

"Yes." Giovanna smiled. "Archibald wanted to preserve the hillside, live with it and not just on it. He constructed it so that the house molded into the landscape. It provides natural insulation and protection. It's quite brilliant."

"You live inside a hill?" sneered Radu. "Like a badger?"

"Big talk from a Gypsy living out of a trunk," I said.

"Bastard!" Radu kicked the back of the seat hard enough to crush me into the steering wheel.

"Son of a bitch!" I reached behind and grabbed him by the hair and slammed his head on the box of canned goods next to him.

"BOYS!" Giovanna screamed and pulled me off him. Despite her condition, her strength was still amazing. "We don't have time for this childishness! Jake, please! I don't know how much longer before." She looked back at Radu. "Before I won't be able to help you against You Know Who."

"You know who who?" asked Radu. "What kind of trouble are you in now, Janos?"

"Never mind," I said. "Let's get unpacked."

As we pulled boxes out of the car, a tall dark-skinned man rushed out to meet us. He was wearing dark work pants, a stained beige undershirt and suspenders.

"Mrs. Bonham! We did not receive any return message that you were coming!"

"I'm sorry, Vincent. It was a change of plans."

"I am so happy that you are here. Please excuse how I appear, madam, we are working on the plumbing. Master Arthur is very handy with a wrench, madam. He has been quite helpful."

Giovanna stopped in her tracks. "Arthur?"

"Yes, madam, I sent you several telegrams. It's a miracle! I assumed that is why you are here."

Giovanna broke away from us and ran into the house.

"Well, this will be a wonderful Christmas," said Vincent, stepping in front of me. "To have Master Arthur back in the house."

"Yes, well, I need to get these boxes inside."

He continued blocking my entrance. "I'm Vincent. My wife, Miranda, and I are the caretakers here. We've been in service with the Bonham family for twenty years." He pointed a small .22 at me. "Who are you, please?"

"Jake Istenhegyi. I'm a friend of Mrs. Bonham. I've been driving since six a.m. and I'd like to freshen up."

Vincent kept up the block. "And who is he?"

I looked back at my half-brother. He was filthy and he smelled like two weeks of dirty laundry. His swollen black eye was a crusty mess and he tried to smile with a busted lip.

"That? Oh, he's just a stray we picked up on the way." I pushed the box into Vincent's chest and relieved him of his gun. "You know what a soft touch Madam is towards the down and out. Maybe she'll have you give him a job cleaning the gutters."

Seeing Radu's pout was worth nearly getting shot.

*****

The front room was decorated for the holidays. A large tree, heavy with ornaments stood in the corner. On the floor next to it was a nativity scene. Mother Mary kneeling at the manger, staring beatifically at the babe inside. I didn't know if it was the heat from the fire in the hearth or the heavy log crossbeams in the ceiling overhead that gave the illusion the room was collapsing in on me,

Or it might have been the sight of Giovanna sobbing as she hugged her son, Arthur.

He was taller than his mother but other than that they could've been twins. Raven hair and dark eyes, tall and thin. He looked rather good for a soldier who was killed in Flanders Field fifteen years earlier.

"Jake! Come and meet my son, Arthur. Sweetie, this is my friend, Jake. He helped me get home."

The young man shook my hand, but his eyes looked away from mine. "Hello, suh-sir," he stammered. "A friend of my muh-mother's is a friend of mine."

"Good to hear."

"Hello, I'm--" Radu held out his hand.

"He's someone we picked up looking for work as a handyman."

"What?" Radu stared at me, slack jawed.

I patted Vincent on the shoulder and palmed back his gun. "Vincent, could you get him settled in?"

Vincent stood still and waited for Giovanna to nod her approval before taking Radu back to the kitchen. Radu made a finger motion I'm too much of a gentleman to repeat but I'm not going to lie and say I didn't think the same thing right back at him.

"Giovanna, I hate to interrupt but we are on a schedule."

"Oh, yes, yes," she said, wiping away a tear. She held her son's face. "I have something important to do in the lab but promise me you won't disappear. You'll still be here later?"

"I'm nuh-not going anywhere, Mama. The qu-question is where have you been?"

"I was gone but now I'm back." She kissed his face and hugged him desperately, as if trying to remember every fold of him. "And I'm not going away, ever again, so help me God."

*****

There wasn't time for the ten-cent tour of the house. I followed her straight back to the kitchen and to a locked metal door that would've looked more at home in a medieval castle. She retrieved two flashlights from a pantry and gave me one.

"Watch your head," Giovanna said. "It gets bumpy from here."

The door opened to a dark hallway. I turned on my flashlight and scanned the walls. Adobe brick. The beam of my light fell on another door ahead of us.

"Why so many doors? Security?"

"It creates a safety zone, a cushion between the lab and the house. Explosions do happen."

The second door was another slab of metal. No keyhole, no handle. In the center was a square filled with shapes with one empty space; a puzzle box.

"Well, that's different."

"Alchemists are very fond of puzzles and I have lots of secrets to keep."

She asked me to turn around. I did as she moved the puzzle pieces around to unlock the door.

"Clever," I said.

"Wait until you see what lies beyond."

She opened the second door, flipped on a wall light and suddenly I was in Wonderland.

It was a mixture of now and then, Merlin's cave and a scientist's sterile workplace. It had a glass roof attached to an intricate pulley system to open the panes for fresh air. There were bookcases stuffed with volumes of books, some new and others so ancient they looked as if they should've been in a museum. On the shelves were beakers and jars filled with a rainbow of colored liquid. Some contained disfigured creatures, aborted rats or some other experiment that had gone wrong, I guessed. In the center of the room were three long metal tables with beakers and burners and long curlicue tubes that dripped into other beakers. There were machines I don't even know how to describe much less give a name to sitting beside more ancient tomes. At the end of one table was a cage that was covered in a tarp. There were two sinks with faucets, cupboards filled with what I couldn't imagine.

"I thought you mad scientists worked in dark, moldy basement laboratories."

"Hardly. There are three cardinal rules in chemistry: ventilation, ventilation, ventilation. I've seen too many alchemists go mad from mercury fumes."

"What's in the cage?"

She pulled the oil skin flap away to reveal a stone rat, forever captured in the act of grooming its ear. "Jake, meet Rattio. I told you about him, remember?"

"I figured it would have died by now."

"Why? With a regular infusion of the Salt elixir, Rattio is just like us. Unfortunately, I wasn't here to give him a dose. Now, we can use him to test our new serum. Give me your hand."

I held out my right hand. She flipped it and jabbed a syringe into the meaty part of my palm. "Hey!"

"Hold still." She held me fast as she drew blood.

"What the hell?"

"Don't be such a baby. Be grateful for syringes. Back in my day, I would've had to bleed you with a knife and a bowl."

She opened the rat's cage. "Now, watch."

She squirted a drop of my blood onto the stone rat's face. It rolled down its nose until... movement. A quick twitchy motion later, the whiskers bristled and a tiny pink tongue peeked out and lapped at the blood. Seconds later, the rat was shaking as if fresh from the bath, licking and preening its fur.

"Exactly what I expected." She looked at her wristwatch and wrote something in her notepad. "Now, we wait."

"For what?"

Rattio shivered, chirped a small surprised, "Squeak?" and turned to stone.

"Well, that's disheartening," she said. "I hypothesized the topical effects wouldn't last very long but

I just needed to test it out. I'm giving myself two or three more days."

"Giovanna." I put my hands on her shoulders and pulled her to me. She rested against me for a few seconds, nuzzling my chest with her face. I held her like this for a few, sacred moments until she pushed herself away, wiping her eyes.

"Don't worry about me. I have extra incentive now that my Arthur is home."

"I thought he was killed in the war."

"So did we. We never received his body just a letter from the government. Poor Archibald. I know it broke his heart not to be able to give his son a proper burial. But, maybe…maybe the Salt somehow transfused through the uterine wall? Perhaps the stress of his 'death' activated the Salt already present in his system?"

"But where has he been for fifteen years?"

"I don't know. He's been through so much. Just looking at him…in his eyes…he's so thin. And he never had a stammer before the war. I wonder why?" She waved the questions away. "No, I can't think about that right now. I'll tackle those mysteries after I create a new elixir."

"No pressure."

"The good news is that I am great under pressure. So, take off your shirt and lie down on that bed. I'll have Miranda brew some coffee. It's going to be a long night."

CHAPTER TEN

Aces

The life of a lab rat is a boring one.

To pass the time, I read the *Black Mask* magazine I snatched from Bear's office. Or at least I tried to. My eyes kept crossing as I tried to concentrate on the words that kept sliding around on the paper.

"I feel woozy," I said, dropping the magazine to the floor.

"That's normal for as much blood as I've siphoned off you. A normal person would've passed out or worse by now," Giovanna said. She picked up the magazine and gave it back to me. "I'll get you something to eat. You'll feel better after you've had Miranda's spicy--"

I blacked out before I found out what was so spicy about Miranda.

*****

I woke up to the sound of scratching and shuffling and something whirling like a top. In my half-stupor, my first thought was that rats were running amok in the lab. I clenched the magazine as I opened my eyes and in my hazy vision, I saw something tall and dark, rummaging through Giovanna's bookcase.

"Who are you? What are you doing over there?"

The figure turned, slowly. It was Arthur. "You're awake. Good, good." He blushed and pushed the books back into place. "That's good."

The whirling stopped and a series of BEEP BEEP BEEPs followed. It came from a square, white box in which Giovanna had placed all six tubes of my blood. Whatever it was meant to do was finished.

"I think the soup's done," I said. "Where's your mother? She'd want to be here when it comes out of the oven."

"I'll go get her," he said, smiling with too many teeth. There was sweat on his brow and his eyes were wild. You didn't need to be Sherlock Holmes to know this man was terrified...but of what?

And then I felt it again, like before in the alleyway behind the Odyssey Shop. The sharp pulling in my fingers, like magnets of the same polarity calling to each other.

"So, this is the Jake Istenhegyi I've been hearing so much about," a voice said from behind me. "Pity."

It was the man from the Packard. The silver eyepatch told me as much. He stood in the doorway of the lab looking the place over, like an invading king looking over his spoils. He was wearing a gray wool overcoat, Italian cut if I wasn't mistaken, black leather shoes, polished like mirrors, and a white leather glove stained with blood on his right hand. Wavy, dark hair with a tint of silver at the temple. I guess the ladies would call him devilishly handsome even without the patch over his left eye. Personally, the smirk on his full pouty lips made me want to punch him.

"It's always the same, isn't it?" said Lucio Amara as he leaned against the doorway. "People are never as impressive as you imagine them to be."

"I've been told I should be taller." I sat up and the world spinned.

Lucio laughed. "Funny. You're funny. That's good. It will serve you well. A sense of humor. Isn't that right, Arthur?"

He flinched at the sound of his name. "Y-yes."

"Did you find it?" The tall man glided over and raised his gloved hand up to the young man's face.

The young man looked cowed and shook his head. "Not yet. It has to be here. I just…just duh-don't kn-know which book--"

Lucio slapped Arthur with his gloved hand. It sounded like he had socked him with a bag of rocks. The boy went down to the stone floor and collapsed at his feet.

"Hey!" I got off the bed and stood on wobbly legs. "Watch it!"

Lucio held up his hand to me like a traffic guard. With his gloved hand he rubbed the boy's back.

"I'm sorry. So sorry," Arthur mumbled as he kissed Lucio's shoes. "Puh-puh-please sorry sorry let me help let me help you."

My lips pulled back in revulsion as I watched Arthur crawl on the floor like a dog that had its snout rubbed in its own shit. What happened to this boy? And then I remembered. The missing years. Christ. Fifteen years.

"What the hell did you do to him?"

"I merely taught him a valuable lesson. Isn't that right?"

Arthur trembled in agreement as his bladder let go.

"What lesson did you teach him that makes him quake on the floor in his own piss?"

"That there are worse things, so much worse, than death." Lucio helped the boy up to his knees. "Isn't that so, Arthur?"

The boy nodded and pawed at Lucio's leg.

"You can speak, boy."

"Yes, yes so manymanymany things thank you, yes. Let me show you I can be useful." Arthur lurched back to the table full of books, beakers and tools. "I can find it. I can I can I can I can! Let me show you…"

"If only your mother was so compliant."

Arthur stopped. "But you puh-promised you wouldn't hurt her."

"Where is Giovanna?" My hand went to the pistol in my pocket but stopped. I didn't want to expose my only card. "Where is she, you sick son of a bitch?"

"In the bath." Lucio said. "Reconsidering her answers."

"The buh-bath but." Arthur's body shook as if he were a volcano readying to erupt. "You promised me. If I opened the door, you wouldn't hurt her. YOU PROMISED!"

Something snapped inside that broken boy's mind and he charged Lucio, screaming a deep, primal guttural growl. But halfway to his goal, Arthur seized and crumbled to the floor like a ball, frothing and gasping for breath.

"Silly boy," Lucio Amara held out a small stained leather pouch. He squeezed the pouch tightly in his fist and

Arthur screamed and twisted in agony. "Did you forget who owns you?"

"Stop!" I shouted. "You're killing him!"

Lucio's laughter bounced off the walls. "He wishes he could die. Don't you? Speak, Arthur."

"YESYESYESYES! OH GOD PLEASE! ARRRRGH! PLEASE!"

"You son of a bitch. Stop it!" I clenched my fist around the tightly rolled *Black Mask* magazine as I started towards Lucio, ready to punch the smugness out of the bastard.

"That's it. I can't take any more. Leave him alone!"

"Not so fast, Istenhegyi." He draped the pouch over his stiff right hand and held out another one. It was newer. The leather was still dark and not as pliable. He squeezed it, slowly but firmly. My breath caught in my throat and a pain blossomed in my chest.

I stopped and bent over as nausea rolled over me. I tried to take deep breaths, but it felt impossible. It was like my lungs couldn't inflate.

It was the pouch. Christ. I had experiences with pouches. The last one held the shrunken skull of that murderous bitch, Henrietta Harleaux. She used it as a hiding place when she wasn't using her granddaughter, Pearl, as a meat puppet.

He released his grip and the pain immediately ceased. I could breathe and the nausea fell away. I noticed Arthur was also pain free.

"Would you like to know what's in here?"

"Surprise me."

"Your heart."

"Impossible!" He squeezed again and I was down on my knees from the pain.

"You were saying?"

"Where...how?"

"It was a curious business transaction. I only meant to purchase the Cross of Trismegitus, oh, I see you remember that little trinket. Then you know why I wanted it: the sliver of Sal Vitae Aeternam inside the center of the cross. Or, as it turned out, a reasonable facsimile of the Salt."

"It was real," I said, getting to my feet. "I felt it."

"The Elixir it yielded was, frankly, piss. Whether it was of poor quality to begin with or being kept in the hull of scuttled pirate ship in the Louisiana bayou tainted it, the Salt wasn't pure enough to create a potent elixir. Many of the Order are locked in a coma. I was luckier, in a sense, but I have my own complaints. I am now crippled with a stone hand and this."

Amara carefully lifted his eyepatch to show the calcified remains of an eye socket. A dry line of dust leaked down his cheek like tears. He wiped away the detritus and reaffixed the patch.

"It makes perfect sense that God should torture me in this way. I've always been a slave to vanity. But you were asking about your heart. The charming lady who sold me the Cross asked for more than the agreed price because of some trouble she ran into and wanted compensation. I questioned her further and was amazed to learn that she had a run in with someone who could not die. She said she cut out his heart but still, no dice. And even stranger, the heart continued to beat outside his chest.

"That part interested me. 'Do you still have the heart?' I asked her. And, being a savvy businesswoman, she offered it up for a price and a favor. I have it here. Well, most of it. I've had to slice a chunk off for Pacu to use for a spell to track you down in New Orleans. Remember him? Short. Facial tattoos. Sharp teeth. He was a shaman, very skilled in sympathetic magical arts." He gave the pouch a tight squeeze and I gritted my teeth against the pain. "His acolytes will be angry that you killed him."

"What can you do with a heart? It's just a hunk of meat, outside the body."

"The Order sees science and magic as two sides of the same coin. In my time with them, I've learned a few tricks. I was able to use your heart to track you to here after that fiasco in New Orleans."

"And control me. The voice I heard in my head, telling me to stop the car, that was you."

"That was me, yes! Sympathetic magic. Simple, really. Childish compared to other things I've seen. I prefer a more physical approach, as you can tell. Still, imagine my surprise at finding you as well as that murdering whore, Giovanna."

"Don't call her that."

"Oh, didn't you know? How do you think she got the Salt away from her father?"

"She said he died. That there was a fire. She and her sisters barely escaped."

"There was a fire. That is true. But her father died before the fire…when she *strangled* him to steal the Salt. Then your precious Giovanna and her sisters *set* the house on fire. I remember that part very well because I was trapped in a goddamn cell with five other men. She left us there to burn!"

I felt like I'd been kicked in the stomach.

"Oh, your face!" Lucio laughed. "I do love the look a man gets when he realizes the truth about something he thinks is so pure."

"How does Arthur figure into this?"

"The Order has been keeping track of the Lombardi sisters for ages. And when one of them had a child, well, as you can imagine, that created a sensation. We've been watching the boy his entire life. We went so far as to have men go into war with him, to keep him safe and report back to us. When he was shot down, his handlers retrieved the body and had him sent to our home office in Switzerland. He's been in my company ever since. I knew he would be useful someday. After the fiasco with the infusion of the Salt from the Cross of Trismegitus, I sent him here to look for her journals hoping I could glean something to help me but, alas, he failed."

Arthur whimpered a high-pitched whine.

"After all I have done for him. I ask for one simple chore."

Amara kicked the cowering young man in the head, sending him flying backwards where he laid motionless.

It was my turn to break.

Everyone wants to think that, if given the opportunity to be a hero, they'd rise to the occasion in an instant but that's not what happens. The normal response to violence is to shy away, not get the predator's attention, to not get involved because, all in all, most people are content, happy in their own way, and don't want to mess it up by taking on another person's problems.

In short, happy people are never heroes.

I'm no different from anyone else. If you want me to be a hero, find me on a Bad Day. When I'm angry, hurt and have nothing left to lose.

Luckily, today was a very bad day.

"Do yourself a favor, Amara," I said as I slipped my hand into my pocket. The other hand gripped the magazine. "Hand over the pouches and walk away before things get worse."

"Are you serious?" Lucio looked beyond me. "Is he serious?"

"He does have a terribly inflated sense of self," said an imperious feminine voice.

A woman walked in with the shambling zombies of Thomas and Grover Baskerville on leashes behind her. Those poor bastards. They were con men but, in the end, they only kept up the ruse out of misplaced love for their mark, Wayburn Crabtree. I wondered if he was somewhere lurking in the shadows.

"Hello, lover," she cooed.

"Hello, bitch. Still wearing Pearl's face?"

Henrietta Harleaux caressed her granddaughter's cheek. "She suits me nicely. Don't you think so?"

"It's better than the shrunken apple head I tossed into the swamp." I turned to Lucio. "Why is she here?"

"Remember that favor, I mentioned?" Lucio explained. "It was to watch you suffer."

"Ah. Of course, it was."

"She wanted to watch you die but since that's probably not possible, I was able to negotiate it down to suffering."

"Fine, I like an audience. I'll give you one more chance, Amara. Hand over the pouches and walk away or I won't be responsible for the consequences."

Lucio laughed and lightly squeezed the pouch holding my heart. I kept my face firm, biting back the excruciating pain. I wouldn't give him or Harleaux the pleasure of watching me suffer.

"Can you believe the hubris of the men of this age? It is astonishing, truly. I have risen from a thief left to die in a cage to the Supreme Master in the Order of Zosimos. What do you think you, a boy playing at being a detective, can do to me?"

It was true. I didn't have much in my hand. There were only two aces up my sleeve. One of them was the pistol in my pocket and the other one was a dead man.

I had to give it a shot.

I tapped the *Black Mask* magazine on the metal frame of the bed.

Nothing.

Once more. Harder.

"What the hell is he doing?"

Harleaux shook her head and shrugged.

Dammit, Bear!

Third time. *Please. For the love of God. PLEASE!*

The temperature dropped and the ghost of Barrington "Bear" Gunn, inconveniently deceased private detective, appeared in front of me. He looked solid, fresh and full of juice. Even his fedora had a sharp edge.

"Jake? What the hell? Where the hell am I?"

"No time to explain. See that smug asshole in the coat? Grab the pouches out of his hand and leg it!"

"Can do." Bear Gunn, a hulking man of 6' 4" when he was alive towered over the 5' 6" Lucio and snatched the pouches out of his hand. "Thanks kindly," he said, saluted and disappeared.

"What the hell was that?" Lucio demanded.

"Don't complain now," I said, pulling my .38 snub nose out of my pocket. "I gave you a chance to leave. This is all on you."

I only had six bullets. I used the first two on the Baskerville Brothers, dead center in their foreheads. They fell to the ground with barely a sound, like puppets whose strings were cut.

"NO! Istenhegyi, you bastard!" Harleaux roared at me.

I aimed at Harleaux.

"You will not win! I forbid it!" She threw her head back and howled. It sounded like rushing wind pouring through the mouth of a cave. When it was over, her features softened and her granddaughter, Pearl, surfaced.

"Where am I? Oh my God. What happened? What did she do?"

Her eyes focused on my gun. Pearl nodded her head, tears streamed down her face. "Please, Jake. Do it. Kill me. I can't live like this. Please, set me free. My boy. I can be with him, in spirit. He will be safe from her when I am gone."

"Oh, God…no." My hand wavered. "I can't."

She just smiled at me, her caramel eyes begging me, forgiving me.

Damn her.

I aimed and used my third bullet. I'd like to say she had a smile on her face when she fell but I didn't have the stomach to look.

I aimed at Lucio. "You bastard."

He smiled that goddamn smug toothy smile. "You can't kill me."

"No, but I learned something tonight. There are worse things than death."

I lowered the barrel and shot him in the groin.

He fell to the floor, screaming. "You bastard!" He cupped his crotch, blood squeezing out between his fingers. "I'll destroy you! Aaaargh, oh my God. I'll own you!"

"Get in line."

Behind me, I heard laughter. Arthur was sitting cross legged, like a child, and clapping his hands. "Good! Again! Again!"

"I would, kid, if I had the bullets. Come on, let's find your mother."

CHAPTER ELEVEN

The Bath

I figured that Lucio Amara was the kind of guy who would come with an entourage and I found them. Dead in the kitchen. Three shot in the head. Two with their necks sliced open like cantaloupe. Miranda lay on the floor, grasping a knife, dead by gunshot.

"What happened while I was out?"

"I don't know. After I let them in, I went to look for the juh-journals. Master pruh-promised he wouldn't h-hurt her. I didn't know, I promise. This all my fault."

I heard something fall in the hallway.

"Radu? Vincent?" I called out with Arthur hugging close at my heels.

A raspy voice answered from the hallway, "Here."

It was Vincent, gut shot. He smiled up at me as he gripped his stomach together but the pool of blood surrounding him told a fatal story. He was dying and fast.

"Where is Giovanna? Have you seen Radu?"

"Madame is in the pool," he managed to croak out.

"Help her." And he was gone.

"The bath." Arthur's voice trembled as he whispered and then rushed away.

I followed him down a hallway to the indoor pool. I could see Giovanna, weighted down by buckets of cement. She was naked and her short hair floated like a black halo crowing her head.

"Mama!" Arthur screamed and jumped in the pool. I dived in and we both swam down to her. He struggled to untie the thick rope tied around her waist and I worked on the knots that held her to the buckets. We both pulled her to the surface.

She lay in a fetal position on the brick floor by the pool. There were bruises on her face, her back and her neck. An ear had been sliced off. Two of her fingernails had been ripped out. That son of a bitch had tortured her before tossing her into the pool to slowly drown. If she were anyone else, anyone *normal*, she would be dead, long past any hope of recovery. But I knew different. She wasn't dead, more in a coma while the Salt left in her body worked to repair the damage and restore her to life. I just hoped she had enough left in her system to finish the job.

"Move out of the way," Arthur said, his voice firm and confident. The stature of the young man transformed in the blink of an eye. Gone was the beaten dog from only minutes before.

Arthur started beating her back like a drum until Giovanna vomited out a rush of pool water.

"Good trick," I said.

"I have lots of experience in this. The Bath is one of Master's favorite punishments."

"Jesus. Is she breathing?"

"Barely. What is that on her stomach, a rash? It's creeping down her legs."

The gray blemish was growing. The stress of drowning was quickly using up whatever Salt my blood had transferred to her. Within the hour, she'd be more stone than woman.

"We need to get her warm," I said.

On the wall, there was a circular rack of a dozen towels, rolled up like logs. Keeping Giovanna warm wasn't going to do squat if she turned into a planter in front of our eyes but I didn't want to tear away whatever hope Arthur had left. I didn't have the heart to do that to the kid.

I grabbed one and the rack spun like a wheel. That's when inspiration struck.

"Here, take the towels. Keep her safe. I'll be right back."

"Where are you going?"

"I have an idea."

*****

I ran back to the lab, my wet shoes sliding on the blood in the floor and rushed over to the strange white box with the blinking lights. I didn't what it was or what it did; lab rats aren't given a lot of information.

I flipped two metal latches that kept the top closed. The lid opened and inside were six test tubes in a circle, like a merry-go-round. I plucked out a tube. The blood inside had separated. A clear watery liquid on top and red, thicker liquid on the bottom. I shook the tube and heard knocking, like tiny stones. There wasn't any time for scientific decorum. I found a piece of gauze, covered the mouth of the test tube and poured it out onto the table.

"Please, please, please," I muttered under my breath and looked into the gauze.

There it was. Three small crystal balls. Were these seeds? What Giovanna needed to make a new Salt of Life crystal? I didn't know and had no time to find out.

I held the gauze tight in my hand and went back to the kitchen. Stepping over bodies, I found a coffee cup and filled it with water from the sink. I poured the small crystal balls into the cup and they quickly dissipated.

Is that it?

Just then, the front door slammed and seconds later the sound of a car burning rubber as it sped away.

Lucio! It hit me. He wasn't in the lab, just a pool of blood that I slipped in. *Dammit!*

No time to deal with his escape or to wonder where the hell Radu was hiding. IF he was hiding. No time. I had to get back to the pool and fast.

*****

Arthur had Giovanna wrapped up in towels from head to toe.

"Is she awake?"

Arthur shrugged. "She comes and goes."

"Sit her up. We need to get this down her throat."

He positioned her between his legs and leaned her back against his chest.

"Giovanna, honey, can you hear me?"

She moaned softly.

"Listen to me. I need you to drink this." I opened her mouth and slowly poured the water into her mouth. "I think it will help." She drank it slowly and, thankfully, didn't spit any back up. "But don't get your hopes up; I'm a lousy bartender."

I trickled the last few grainy drops in her mouth, waited and prayed.

Nothing happened.

"Come on, baby." I rubbed her leg as if I was trying to put life back into her gray skin. Fear tasted like bile in the back of my throat. Was it strong enough? Too strong? Was it even the Salt? Did I just force poison down her throat? Christ! My breath was ragged with anticipation.

"You can do it," I said, trying to sound cheerful. "Come back, Giovanna."

"Please, Mama," Arthur whispered in her ear. "Come back to me."

She grimaced once and then a pink blush started in her face, erasing the bruises, rebuilding her ruined ear. It radiated down her throat, across her chest and ran down the rest her body like paint. She clenched her hands into fists and then released. The missing fingernails grew back, slowly, until they matched the others. The gray scaly flesh on her stomach and legs fell away like dead leaves and turned to dust. She took a deep breath and arced her back, groaning in intoxicated frenzy as the Salt burned through her veins. I remembered that feeling and I envied her.

When it was over, she lay in her son's lap, panting from exhaustion and ecstasy.

"Mama?"

Giovanna opened her eyes, shining and dark, and reached up to stroke his face. "Hello, baby."

I finally breathed. "It worked. It did, right? It worked?"

Giovanna looked at me as if she had forgotten I was there. "What did you do?"

I told her about the white box, the test tubes, the little rocks. "Was that okay?"

"I'll need to do some more tests but, yes. The initial tests seem to be conclusive. My friend, we have a new seed crystal. Or at least we had one."

"There were other tubes. Five others. One of them must have more crystals."

"Perhaps. Let's go and see but, first," she said, holding the towel to her chest. "Can I get some clothes? And is anyone else starving?!"

CHAPTER TWELVE

Clean Up

Giovanna retired to her room to dress. Arthur stood beside me in the kitchen. I looked at the carnage in the kitchen and thought of the bodies in the lab and realized at a time like this, I really missed Mama Effie's cleanup crew.

"Your mother wouldn't have an incinerator handy?" I asked him.

Arthur shook his head.

"A backhoe?"

He shrugged.

"Industrial grade acid?"

His face lit up. "Yes! Practically a pool of it."

"Excellent." Then a question rolled across my mind. "Do you have any idea why?"

"I never thought to ask."

"Knowing your mother, it's probably best not to know. Show me where."

He led me to a hallway that ran nearly a half a mile into the hillside, away from the lab. Another metal door led to a room with a 6' x 10' metal tank. A steel ladder curled around one side and on the other there was a mechanized lift. The smell burned the inside of my nose and I wondered if I'd ever smell anything again.

"I'll help you drag the bodies," said Arthur.

"No. Thanks for the offer but your mother needs you. Make her plate, grab a bottle of wine, and take care of her. I'll clean up this mess."

Arthur smiled, relieved. "Thanks. I owe you."

We walked back through the laboratory and I stopped at the bodies of Pearl and the Baskerville Brothers. The thought of melting her in acid made my stomach turn. "Do you have any other ideas for a more proper burial?" I asked Arthur. "Vincent and Miranda, for instance."

Arthur bit his lower lip. "The conservatory, maybe? My father was a brilliant botanist. He created an entire ecological habitat in his conservatory. After he died, Vincent and Miranda stayed behind mainly to keep it alive. It's a beautiful piece of Eden, I've always thought. Perhaps, burying them in one of those plots?"

"Excellent idea. Show me where it is and point me to a shovel."

****

Dragging goons with no names to the acid bath and dumping them inside was physically draining but it was nothing compared to the emotional toil of burying friends.

Arthur was correct in calling his father's conservatory Eden. It was a fantastic place of eternal spring and summer. Underground steam kept the room at a perfect temperature. Exotic plants and flowers I have never imagined bloomed and small birds and insects flew around my head. A small beehive buzzed in the corner. It was an intact universe, pure and simple. A perfect place to lay my friends to rest.

I buried Thomas and Grover Baskerville in a patch of flowers that were labeled 'Calla Lily Night Caps'. They reminded me of trumpets the street musicians I'd seen in New Orleans play. I thought they'd appreciate it.

I didn't know Vincent or Miranda very well but I buried them nearest to the beehives near a patch of purple flowers with no tag. It felt right.

And Pearl. My poor doomed Pearl. I wanted to give her the perfect resting place. I wandered around the conservatory until I found it. A bush of purple roses so dark they almost seemed black. I wished I had a more poetic tongue so that I could say something eloquent over her grave but…this was the best I had to offer. Rest in Peace, Pearl.

*****

I pulled out a bucket and mop and looked at the mess of blood and gore in the kitchen. My back hurt from dragging corpses and digging holes. I needed help but I didn't want to interrupt Giovanna's reunion. Radu had to be around here somewhere, hiding from good, honest work so I went to look for him.

I passed by Giovanna's room. She and Arthur were sitting on the bed, talking. Their voices were low, nearly a whisper. Arthur started sobbing and she stroked his hair and kissed him on the forehead. He fell into her lap, crying, and she leaned over him, holding him, shielding him from all the demons living inside his head.

My throat went dry and I walked away, quickly. I felt dirty, like a peeping Tom outside watching an intimate scene behind a closed window. I also felt another emotion. Jealousy. I hoped Arthur appreciated what he had.

I checked the other rooms Radu could be hiding and found nothing. Where the hell was he?

I went back to the kitchen and grabbed the mop, resigned to being the Cinderella in this fairytale.

Someone tapped me on the shoulder.

"Radu, you lazy bastard." I slammed the mop back into the bucket. I turned to face him and hear whatever fantastic lie had to tell. "Where the hell--?"

I stopped. It was Lucio.

"Radu left hours ago. I think he stole your car." Lucio said and slugged me with his stony right hand. I saw stars and fell to the floor then he kicked me dead center in the gut until I folded like an empty wallet. I gasped and did my best to hold down my vomit as he kicked me again and again.

"Who do you think you are dealing with?! Who do you think you are to me?!? You are nothing!"

I instantly thought of Giovanna and Arthur, unguarded, unprepared. I grabbed his foot and held on like a dog to its last bone. "Maybe but I won't let you hurt them anymore!"

Lucio stumbled, caught himself, slammed his knee into my chest and smashed his rock of a fist into my face. I felt my nose break. Stars exploded and my left eye was crushed into jelly and my skull cracked open.

Before the blackness enveloped me, I heard him whisper, "Tell Giovanna the Order thanks her."

And then nothing.

CHAPTER THIRTEEN

Merry Christmas, Jake Istenhegyi

It was the itching at the tip of my nose that woke me up. I reached to scratch and felt the rough texture of gauze. Feeling further down my cheeks, it was everywhere. My entire head was wrapped as tight as a mummy.

"MMmmmrgh!" I panicked and started tearing at my face, desperate to breathe.

"Slow down, son," a comforting dark baritone voice said. "Let me get some help."

Moments later, a soft hand caressed mine. Giovanna.

"It's okay, Jake. I'll cut away the bandages. Be still."

A few snips later and I was free. Giovanna, smiling and radiant, sat beside me on an unfamiliar bed. Arthur, looking hardier as if a spark inside him had been relit, stood beside her. Bear, looking a bit ragged on the edges, stood behind him.

"Bear? How did you get here?"

"The boy here." He waved the *Black Mask* magazine and nodded towards Arthur. "He's a fast learner. Called me up and I've been here ever since."

"How long have I been out?"

"Ten days," said Arthur. "How do you feel?"

"Weird, kind of dizzy, like I've been on a merry-go-round."

"No wonder!" Arthur's voice was full of excitement. "You were a mess. You should've seen it! It was fascinating to watch your bones reassemble and your eyes reform. I can only imagine what your brain was doing inside your skull! The Salt is fascinating. I can't wait to do more experiments with it!"

"I'm glad I could help. What happened?" I asked. "My memory is fuzzy."

"You had your head bashed in," said Bear. "Like someone dropped a boulder on it."

"In a sense, he did." My last memory rushed at me and I sat upright, making my head swim. "Lucio! He's still here!"

Giovanna shushed me and pushed me down, gently. "Be calm. He's gone now."

"He didn't try anything after I ...after I was out, did he?"

"No," she said, smiling sadly.

"Then how did you know he was here?"

"By his calling card. He left it inside the centrifuge." She showed me the postcard. It had a picture of a fountain and the words 'Wish you were here!' on it.

"It's an inside joke," she explained. "My father's house was where that fountain is today."

"Ah. He took the other vials?"

"Oh, yes. And all of my journals that he could carry. The rest he tossed into the acid vat after destroying my laboratory."

"So, he has everything he needs to create more Salt?"

"Yes, but what he doesn't have is this." She tapped her temple. "I have centuries of scientific exploration that he can't even begin to comprehend. And I have you. The purest font of Salt on the planet. I will build again, and my new elixir will be stronger than anything he can imagine. But first, I'll need you to roll up your sleeve."

I sighed. "And so it begins."

*****

Three days later, it was Christmas Eve and Giovanna found me in the conservatory visiting Pearl's grave. It bothered me that I didn't feel anything other than a slight twinge of remorse. I barely remembered what she looked like. Perhaps having your brain scrambled and reassembled does that to a man.

"I'm sorry for your loss, Jake."

"I didn't know her, really," I said. "I just understand what it's like being a pawn."

"So why are you going back?" She put her head on my shoulder. "You could stay here with us."

"I don't think I could, to be honest."

"Why?"

"For two reasons. I need you to tell me the truth. Lucio told me you killed your father. Did you leave men to burn to death in cages?"

Giovanna lifted her head from my shoulder, walked a few steps away, stopped and turned to me. Her face was lowered, and her voice was heavy. "I told you before that there were things I did, in another life, that I would never do now. I'm not that woman anymore. Archibald and Arthur, they were my rebirth, my redemption."

"That's all I needed to know."

"So, you'll stay?"

I shook my head. "The second reason. The Odyssey Shop will come for me and the last thing you want is those bastards gunning for you. Besides, Arthur needs you, all of you, if he is ever going to feel whole again. I'm just in the way."

"I'm not going to beg. Do as you will but know this: you will always have a home here with us." She handed me a small gold box with a red bow. "Merry Christmas, Jake Istenhegyi."

I shook the box. "Is this what I think it is?"

"Keep it safe. In a hundred years or so, you're going to need it."

"And I didn't get you anything."

She kissed me on my cheek. "You gave me back my life."

*****

I left the next day while the warm and fuzzies were still fresh. I drove home alone; Bear had dropped off the face of the Earth again. Ghosts are a fickle bunch.

I had a lot of time to ruminate and reflect over everything that had happened to me in the last six months. A lot of it was terrible and traumatic. I had lost friends and more than a little bit of my innocence but the trade-off in the end was worth it. I had found a purpose, as odd as it was, and, in a sense, a family.

I was feeling optimistic about the future as I pulled up to the Odyssey Shop and happy with life right up until a strange man pointed a gun at yours truly.

CHAPTER FOURTEEN

The Year of Jake: Loose Ends

"You're a hard man to find, Jake," the man with the gun says to me. He is slight but muscular, the same height as me. Two fingers on each hand carry gold rings. His suit is not cheap nor expensive, somewhere in the middle. His wears a fedora but I can see graying blonde hair that needs a cut. His face is narrow, his lips in a perpetual frown. Pale blue eyes that never seem to blink. He is, in a word, intense. "And a dangerous one, if I have my facts right."

"Do I know you?"

"Do you recognize this?"

I recognize it immediately despite the scorch marks. It is the license plate from my car that burned in Harleaux's barn.

"Where did you get this?"

"Uh-huh. I thought you would. You know where I found it. And what else I found in there."

"Who are you?"

"Someone that has come a very long way to tie up some loose ends."

The End

JAKE ISTENHEGYI:

THE ACCIDENTAL DETECTIVE

Corpses, Coins, Ghosts and Goodbyes

For my Mother, who always let me be weird

CHAPTER ONE

Around and Around

Here we go again.

I am up to my knees in swamp muck, my hand bleeding into the filthy water, and staring down a crazy woman who wants to kill me.

It feels like a Tuesday.

My name is Jake Istenhegyi and, if you're reading this, you know that I have a natural talent at making poor life choices.

But I never expect any to get me into a war.

CHAPTER TWO

Bishop, Goons and Golems

"You're a hard man to find, Jake," the man with the gun said to me. "And a dangerous man, if I have my facts right."

He was slight but muscular, the same height as me. His suit wasn't cheap, somewhere in the middle. Under his fedora, I saw graying wavy, blonde hair that needed a cut. A narrow face with lips in a perpetual frown. Pale blue eyes that never seem to blink. He was, in a word, intense.

And the .38 in his hand didn't soften his image.

"Who the hell are you?" I said.

"Someone who has come a very long way to tie up some loose ends. My name is Raymond Bishop. I'm a private detective from Los Angeles. Tell me, do you recognize this?"

He held up a piece of metal. I recognized it immediately despite the scorch marks.

"It's a license plate."

"Care to guess whose car it belongs to?"

"I don't need to. It's mine."

"Good to know I'm working with an honest man. Want to explain why I found it in a burned-out barn?"

The wheels in my brain turned so fast I was surprised smoke didn't come out of my ears. I decided to play close to the truth. "I can explain. See, my business partner, Barrington Gunn, borrowed my car to go and check out a lead on a missing person case. Son of a bitch, he told me it was stolen." I gave him my most sincere smile. "Well, I guess he's got some explaining to do."

"Uh-huh. Makes sense." He returned my smile, but his eyes stayed cold. "What about this?"

He held up a pair of scaly legs with four-inch spurs and three gut ripping claws. I knew it intimately. What Raymond Bishop dangled from his fingertips were all that was left of Henrietta Harleaux's monster chicken god. I left it roasting alongside her corpse and the rotting remains of all the men she killed. Among the dead inside that barn was my best friend, Bear, but I couldn't lay that sin on her head; I pulled the trigger that killed him.

"Now *that*…" I said. "Well, that is going to be a little harder to explain."

"Why don't you give it a good college try?"

Before my brain had a chance to conjure up a sane enough whopper to explain away the chicken monster claws, I heard a deep baritone call out. "Jake! Welcome back!"

The voice came from a fat man in a tailored suit standing in the doorway of the Odyssey Shop. Balding and tipping the scales around 300 pounds, I'd have guessed him as one of Mama Effie's better dressed goons except that this one was gifted with the power of speech.

"Do I know you?" I asked.

He smiled warmly and rubbed his hands together. "This cold air isn't good for anyone's health. Come inside and let's get better acquainted."

"Sounds like a plan to me." I tipped my fedora. "Good afternoon, Mr. Bishop."

"Now, hold it one hot damn minute," Bishop said, pulling me in closer, his gun poking me in the back. "I've been looking for this man for weeks. You can have him when I'm done with him."

"Do you have a warrant for his arrest?" The smile on the Fat Man's face never wavered. "Or even a badge?"

Bishop's grip loosened.

"Just a gumshoe, huffing and bluffing your way through life. "Release Istenhegyi."

Bishop renewed his grip. "In a pig's eye!"

"You act as if that is a request." The Big Guy's smile vanished. He snapped his fingers and six goons with chiseled chin good looks appeared behind him and stood silently, awaiting orders.

The goons descended on us in a matter of seconds. One yanked me out of Bishop's grip with such force I was lucky he didn't break my damn arm. "Hey, watch it!" I shouted and then realized I'd seen those chiseled good looks before.

Piera's Valentinoesque golems.

"Bring me Istenhegyi," the Fat Man commanded. "Kill the other one."

"Wait. Did I just hear him tell those guys to kill me?" said Bishop.

"Your ears are working. I hope you fight as big as you talk," I said. "It's gonna get hairy."

I swept my leg under the one who held me, bringing it down. I straddled on its chest and pounded its head into the pavement until the skull cracked open and it stopped moving. I pulled my arm out of its grip.

Bishop was holding his own first emptying his .38 into one and using the license plate like a blade on another. I saw him reach out to grab its face and then pull back yelling, "What the holy hell?!?"

The golem who had tackled Bishop swiveled its head towards me. It was missing a nose. Bishop held out his hand to me and shouted, "What the hell are these things?!?!"

Before I could answer, a silver two-toned Deluxe 8 Packard came screaming around the corner to a dead stop beside us.

The driver was a dame wearing black gloves and a big red hat. The only other part of her I could see was her legs and they were a good enough calling card. Mama Effie was riding shotgun.

"Get in, fools!" said Mama Effie.

I reached for the car door handle and remembered: The Seed. It was in the red box in the front seat of my car. There was no guarantee I'd ever find another one and without it, I would be as good as a golem, a soul trapped into a hunk of stone.

"Wait! I need to get something from my car."

"No time!" Bishop didn't wait to be introduced, opened the door, and pushed me into the backseat. The doors shut as the gas pedal was slammed to the floor and the car's tires squealed down the cold asphalt.

"I do like a man who takes action, stranger," said Mama Effie, winking at Bishop. She was dressed to the nines in a tight jade number that hugged her lean silhouette like a shadow. She had eyeshadow and her fingernails painted to match. Nobody out dressed Mama Effie, even if she was running for her life.

Bishop looked through the rear window at the goons running after the car.

"What the hell were those things?" he huffed. He unclenched his fist and held up a nose that could've been crafted by Michelangelo. Hell, if these were anything like Piera's playthings, it probably had been. "WHAT THE HELL IS THIS?"

"That's something else that will be a bit hard to explain," I said. "How much do you know about golems?"

"What?"

"Golems. Stone men animated by magic."

"What? No. No. Look, I just…can you tell me…golems?" Bishop's face turned red as he stuttered. *"WHAT THE HELL IS GOING ON?!?!"*

"You shouldn't tease him," said the woman in the hat. She had dark brown eyes and ruby red lips the same shade as the ridiculous hat. Middle aged, around 40, but her thick dark hair resisted any streaks of gray. She looked disturbingly familiar. "Janos, it's very rude,"

A lump dropped into my stomach. It hit me. She was the woman in the photograph that was in the letter Radu gave me.

She looked up in the rearview mirror and winked at me.

"Szia, fiam." *Hello, son.*

"What, who…why…HOW?" It was my turn to stammer.

Mama Effie swiped at me with her long, lethal fingernails. "Show some respect! She just saved your ass, boy."

"Thank you, Effie."

"Szívesen, Simza."

"Great. You're teaching her Hungarian. Perfect."

"Hey," interjected Bishop. "I really hate to break up this family reunion but WHAT THE HELL IS GOING ON?"

"Good question." I leaned over the front seat. "What the hell is going on, Mama Effie?"

"The Odyssey Shop is under new management," she said. "And I'm getting the hell out of town."

CHAPTER THREE

Oh, Sugar...

We parked outside a building squeezed into a row of other tall stone facades on Basin Street. Fourteen white marble steps led up to the dog-toothed archway that made me think we were being led into the mouth of a hungry beast. Behind it was a red mahogany door inlaid with a Tiffany styled glass window bursting with gold, red and cobalt blue. Mama Effie knocked three times, paused, and knocked twice more. The door was opened by a tall man in a butler suit.

"Madame," he said. "We were not expecting you."

"Hello, Elliot." Mama Effie gave a quick nod. "*Icarus*."

Elliott stiffened at the word, nodded curtly, reached into his pocket, and handed her a key.

"Thank you. Your service has been appreciated. Please see Mr. Tolliver at the bank for your severance package."

"Very good, ma'am."

The first floor was a very lush reception area with a well-stocked bar and a small stage where a jazz band entertained a small crowd of smartly dressed men and beautiful women. A carpeted staircase led clients to the second floor. Mama Effie escorted us to a small elevator that took us to her private rooms on the upper floor.

Mama Effie's personal suite had a sitting room, a bedroom and a bathroom. The rooms were all lavishly furnished as if to accommodate a courtesan of Louis XVI. Plush, burgundy velvet drapes and colorful wallpaper depicting men on eternally jumping horses on the hunt with the fox always a step ahead. In the bedroom, a massive canopy bed draped in white and gold silks. Did I say courtesan? Strike that. This was a parlor for a queen.

Simza sat at the grand piano, tapping out a quiet melody. I couldn't bring myself to think of her as 'mother'; she was a stranger to me. Yet I couldn't stop sneaking looks, seeing bits and pieces of my own image in her face. My dark eyes. My mouth. We also shared that habit I had of arching my right eyebrow when something amused me. She had musical talent that had, unfortunately, skipped me.

Bishop sat uncomfortably on a spindly chair with legs that creaked whenever he shifted his weight. He was settling his nerves with a glass of something amber and so strong I could smell it from across the room. "What kind of safehouse is this?" he asked. "A whorehouse?"

"It's a boarding house, sir." replied Mama Effie. "Whatever they do to raise their rent money is none of my affair."

Bishop tossed his drink back and went for another one. "Fair enough. I'm not here to hustle a bunch of working women. As long as I can keep him close," he said, pointing at me. "I don't give a damn whose ass they are spanking."

"He's charming," said Simza. "Tell me, do you associate with people of his high class often, my son?"

"For the record, I don't even know this asshole," I said. "I get out of my car and this son of a bitch sticks a gun in my face, and tries to kidnap me."

"Hey! I resent that accusation! It was a citizen's arrest. I have plenty of evidence that you're a dirty -"

"Dirty what? What do you have? Because I can tell you, it's a not a strong upper cut."

"It was an ambush! And I damn near broke my hand on that thing's jaw."

"Jaw? Please. You were throwing wild card punches like a schoolgirl."

"*Boys.*" Mama Effie's frigid tone splashed cold water on our words. She leaned against the marble mantle and crossed her arms. "Are you two are finished or do I need to get a ruler out so we can finish this pissing contest?"

With a steel look, we were both chastened into silence.

"Two weeks ago, I received a telegram from the owners. Long story short: they had sold their share of the Odyssey Shop to new management. Imagine that. The Odyssey Shop sold off like a common whore. Unbelievable. I was told to help with the transition. Make them comfortable." Mama Effie sneered and poked at the burning logs in the fireplace. "The moment that fat bastard walked in the door, I knew it was all going to end in tears.

"They shut everything down. No exporting, no importing. Completely dismantled the business from top to bottom. The fat man, Onofrio Galante, questioned me for days.

"He had only had one interest: finding Jake Istenhegyi."

"Jesus." A thought struck me. Barrington Gunn Investigations had an office on the third floor. "What about Bear? Did they ask about him?"

Mama Effie shook her head. "They only cared about you."

"Have you seen Bear?"

"Once or twice, wandering around the hallway upstairs or just standing there, staring down. I looked right into his eyes. There was nothing looking back at me. Made the hair on my arms stand straight up."

"Wait, you told me that Gunn was out on sabbatical," said Bishop.

"I lied, sweetie," said Mama Effie. "Try and keep up.

"I'm going to need another drink," said Bishop.

"There were a thirteen, at first. Old, sickly men. All they ever ate was watery gruel." Mama Effie grimaced as she remembered. "Disgusting. A waste of my culinary talents. And they brought with them those abominations."

"Wait, what did you mean, there were thirteen *at first*?" asked Bishop.

"They started disappearing. One or two fewer at breakfast. One or two even fewer at dinner. Soon, it was down to only Galante, who never ate anything, and the one in a wheelchair, Vicenzo Barone.

Mama Effie shuddered and her face wrinkled up into a grimace.

"He was the worst of them all. A shrunken, stick of a man. But, oh, Sweet Mother of Christ, that chair.

"Let me tell you that was the strangest wheelchair I have ever seen. It was made from brass, with rubber tubing that went in and out. The thing encased his whole lower body; only his chest from the nipples up, arms and head were visible. And the noises it made! Sweet Lord. Horrible wheezing, gurgling sounds, like a clogged percolator. And worse, it leaked. I had to clean up after it and, I swear to the Holy Mother, Jake…it was blood. That chair leaked blood.

"As luck would have it, I was asked to inventory the remaining stock we had in the room downstairs that we used as a warehouse. Remember the utility room, Jake?"

In the early days of Prohibition, hidden under the Odyssey Shop, was a speakeasy/bordello that serviced the finest of New Orleans high society. On the walls were lurid and incredibly detailed murals of the services the girls would perform for a price. When the glory days were over, my uncle who originally owned the Odyssey Shop, went into debt to some shady entrepreneurs who then used it as an import/export business whose motto took the sign that hung over the doorway, *We Go to the Ends of the Earth to Satisfy Your Needs!* to a different, darker level. All things, esoteric and occult, could be had within these walls. When my uncle decided he no longer wanted to be a part, his shadowy owners decided to call in his debt….and threw him under the wheels of a bus. Upon his death, the debt was inherited by my father who then tossed it off to Yours Truly. So, yes. I remember.

"The stage was curtained off but there were long hoses snaking out from under the fabric and leading down underneath to the orchestra pit. Unfortunately, there were golems standing guard, so I had to bide my time to investigate.

"Shortly after Christmas, things took a turn. A man with an eyepatch rushed into the store and caused a ruckus, demanding to see Barone."

"Eyepatch?" Pieces were starting to fall into place, and I didn't like picture it was forming. "Was his name Lucio Armana? Is he still here?"

"We were never properly introduced." Mama Effie shrugged. "Barone's men took him away. I haven't seen him since."

"Damn." I rubbed my eyes. "This is bad."

"Then we had an earthquake."

"Wait, a what?"

"That's what it felt like. Underneath the store. The whole building shook. The next day, I was told my services were no longer needed and told to vacate. Later that evening, I saw Galante, Barone and most of their monsters leaving so I took my chance and broke into the utility room."

Mama Effie took a deep breath and walked over to the bar. She poured herself a shot of whiskey and tossed it back.

"The things I saw down there."

She poured another shot.

"Good Lord, woman! What!?" said Bishop, exasperated. "What did you see?!"

She tossed back her drink. "Behind the curtains, there were twelve sarcophagi, set up in a half moon formation linked together with pulsating, thick black hoses. In the middle, there was a steel table with straps next to a machine with more hoses. All the tubes led to a hole under the table, center stage. There was a horrible sucking sound, just like the old man's wheelchair. And the stink! I could taste it, like copper in my mouth. I opened the one on the end, just enough to get a peek, and inside was a naked body, shrunken, dried up like an apple that's been left out on the shelf too long. I thought it was a mummy but then it moaned. Its eyelid fluttered and fell away like a butterfly wing."

She poured another shot and her hand shook.

"Jesus..." said Bishop.

"What did you do?" I asked.

"I slammed the lid and ran like a scared rabbit." She downed the shot. "I wasn't thinking. I just ran under the stage. There I found a tank. All the hoses from the stage above led into the tank. The smell was thicker and I could hear something swishing around inside. And then I heard something else. Crying, sobbing, the most heartbreaking sound. I'll never forget it, God help me. It was coming from behind a door, a storage closet, I think. From beneath the door were hoses that lead to the tank. Before I could look inside, Barone's abominations found me and attacked."

"How did you get away?" I asked.

Mama Effie raised a shot glass to Simza. "I will repay that debt, I swear."

"Pffft, stupid creatures." Simza Tokár made a dismissive sound. "Like most men, easy to control if you know the right words."

"What were you doing there?" I asked.

"I was looking for you, Janos." She didn't look at me. She just kept playing the damn piano. I felt a rage deep inside my stomach blossom.

"But why? Why now?" I felt my pale skin blush. My hands clenched into fists. "Twenty-five years, not a word and now, suddenly, you're interested in where I am?"

The melody stopped. "Do you think that I didn't know where you were? I am your mother, Janos. Since the day I birthed you, to when your bastard father stole you away, and every single day after, that I didn't know where my child was? We are connected, kedvsem. Even a goddamn Istenhegyi can't break a mother's bond to her child."

Her eyes teared up. "But something did. One day, I couldn't feel you. Something had changed."

I unconsciously reached back to touch the back of my neck. They were gone now; they'd disappeared after I drank the elixir of the Salt of Life. It healed everything that was broken including old scars. "The scars on my neck. They bound us together?"

"What? Those? No, they were nothing. You had a fever that wouldn't break so I took you to my mother who used hot glass bubbles on the back of the neck. It's an old tradition to pull the sickness out of a child. No, I'm talking about the bond between every mother and child." She patted her stomach. "The scar we all share."

My navel.

"I sent Radu to find you and give you my letter. He wrote back but he never returned."

"Don't hold your breath. The last time I saw him, he was on his way to Hollywood to find fame and glory on my dime. He even stole my name."

"Oh, that fool! Grandmother warned me but...it's my fault. I loved the boy too much. But you have the coin, yes? He said he gave it to you."

"I lost it."

"*What?!*" Simza seemed to shrink as the air left her body. She clutched the piano as if it were the only thing keeping her head above water.

"Simza, are you ill?" asked Mama Effie.

"I knew something was wrong."

"It was just a lucky charm," I said. "Radu had one too. What's so important about it?"

"It's more than just some lucky charm, Janos. It binds me to the carrier. I give one to all my children.

She took off her glove and held up her left palm. Dark veins, like a web were scratched in the center of her hand.

Mama Effie gasped. "Oh, Simza...."

"It is the possession of someone evil. I feared it was you, Janos."

"Me? Why would I be evil?"

"Well, you are an Istenhegyi after all."

I let the comment slide.

She took a deep breath and slowly slid her hand back into the glove. She winced as if it hurt. She walked over to me, each step solid and purposeful. She was barely five-foot-tall and looked up into my eyes. "Do you understand now why I must find that coin?"

I ran my hands through my hair and I tried to remember the last time I had it. "I kept it in a jacket Radu loaned me when I went into the swamp looking for the Rameau's pirate ship. He was pissed because...yes! I left on a boat that was stolen by...holy Jesus." Cold water splashed down my spine as the answer revealed itself to me. "Henrietta Harleaux. She stole the boat. She must have found it in my jacket. She has it."

"Excellent!" said Simza. "Where do you think she is now?"

"That's a good question," said Bishop. The way he squinted at me caused the hair on the back of my neck to rise. "Where is Henrietta Harleaux?"

"I don't know where she is, now," I said, squaring my shoulders. "The last time I had the pleasure of her company was in New Mexico."

"Bullshit!" Bishop crossed the room in three bounds and pushed his face into mine. "You know damn well that Henrietta Harleaux is dead. I found her and all the rest of those bodies out there in that barn. I'm tired of dancing circles with you, boy, so just come clean."

"Bodies?" Simza gasped. "What are you talking about?"

"I'm a private detective, ma'am. Raymond Bishop. Back in July, the Stiegerson family hired Mr. Gunn to retrieve their son but then never heard another word from him. I was hired by my clients to find out what happened to their investment. Since Mr. Gunn was always 'on sabbatical' according to the staff, I started at the beginning and went out to Harleaux's house.

"You want to explain what I found, Jake? No? Then I'll do the honors. I found a burned-out barn and the corpses and skeletons of over a dozen people. One of them I deduced was Harleaux by the clothing and rings on the fingers. There was a badly burned body tied down to a wheel that was laid over a pit where I found….can we take a guess? More bodies."

"But how is my son responsible for this?"

"I found a wrecked car registered to your boy, Jake. I did a little digging into Mr. Istenhegyi." Bishop pulled out a reporter's notebook from inside his jacket and flipped it open. "First off, turns out, he's not even a licensed investigator but, hey, that's a problem for the licensing board. What I'm interested in are all the people who have ended up dead or just disappeared after crossing his path."

Simza's eyes watered as she looked at me. "Janos, what have you done?"

"Wait a minute…I can explain."

"Other than Henrietta Harleaux, there's Piera Lombardi, disappeared, whose sister, Pia Lombardi, was found dead at the bottom of your staircase. Oh, coincidentally, her body is also missing from the morgue. Then there's your involvement with the rigged boxing scandal involving the Irish Mob. How many people died connected to that? Mr. Brannigan, he doesn't like you too much. He told me he thinks you offed Mallone but, between you and me, what's one less Irishman, am I right?"

"If you'd give me a chance to explain…"

"And then there's the treasure hunter, Wayburn Crabtree. You hooked up with his crew to go out into the swamp to look for a pirate ship but, surprise, surprise, you're the only one to come out of the swamp, Istenhegyi. What happened to Crabtree and the Baskerville Brothers? Lots of boys over at Lafitte's bar want to have a word with you about that. So, adding up all the factors here, I came up with a tidy little sum. You're dirty as sin, Istenhegyi." He slapped his notebook shut like a judge's gavel. "Do yourself a favor and tell the truth."

I stared into Bishop's cold blue eyes. My mother stood beside him, staring at me with a look I couldn't decipher. I didn't even care anymore. The anger I felt earlier had drained me.

"Fine. I'm too tired to even try to lie so, to hell with it. Are you ready for the truth?"

"Oh, sugar, here it comes," Mama Effie said, shaking her head, as she sat down at her writing desk.

"First off, I did not kill Henrietta Harleaux. That claw you had? The one that looked like it something ripped off a pteranodon? That was attached to the thing that killed her after I screwed up her ritual."

"Ritual?" said Bishop. "Bullshit, boy. Sell this to *Weird Tales*. I don't have time for this."

"It gets weird from here on out so hang on to your fedora, Bishop. Bear went out to her place to find the Stiegerson kid but found out that Harleaux would lure men to that cottage and sacrifice them to get favors from her weird, monster chicken god. It was six-foot-tall and dripped acid from its fangs. Yes, the chicken god had fangs. Those skeletons in the pit? One of them, God knows which one, was the Stiegerson boy. That body on the wheel? That was Barrington Gunn. Turns out she'd had a rough month and Harleaux needed an extra sacrifice. Bear was in the wrong place at the right time."

"Wait," Bishop stammered. "I thought…"

"No, he's dead. And I'll take responsibility for his death. I shot him, right between the eyes, after he begged me to put him out of his misery. His ghost, however, haunts the Odyssey Shop."

"Wait….*what?"* Bishop said, completely flustered.

"Your friend, Bear, he is a kisértet?" said Simza.

"What's a kisserteet...that?" asked Bishop.

"Kisértet," I said. "A ghost."

"And you let him suffer? Janos, it is wrong to keep the dead here. How do you stomach such torment?"

"It's not like I'm not keeping him as a pet. Unless I carry a Black Mask magazine with me, he can't leave the building. He's stuck there."

"It's a clause in his lease," said Mama Effie, looking up from her writing. "Lease for Life and a thousand years after. All perfectly legal."

"NO, it's not right." Simza appealed to her friend. "You have to release him, Effie."

"What's the problem?" asked Mama Effie. "He seems content."

"Souls need to be set free from this material world. Imagine that they are like candles, burning lower and lower until they are, POOF, nowhere. It is worse than hell."

Now it made sense. The way he looked ragged on the edges, how he was having a harder and harder time keeping solid and all the times he would disappear completely. Jesus. Bear Gunn was fading away like an old photograph left out in the sun.

"Ghosts? Are you pulling my leg? Bullshit!"

"Is that where you draw the line, Bishop? Ghosts? Because, buddy, I've got some bad news for you, we're just getting started.

"First, let's start with the Lombardi sisters. Did your investigation uncover the fact that they were over 500 years old?"

"You're lying. I've seen photos. The youngest was barely twenty if a day."

"Pia. Yeah, she was a corker. Piera and Giovanna were beauties as well. The sisters kept themselves young by drinking an elixir made from the Sal Vitae Aeternam. Speak Latin? No? It roughly translates as 'the Salt of Life'. It's a crystal about three inches high, blue and green, looks like a ziggurat. It takes a hundred years to grow from a seed crystal."

"A seed?" asked Simza.

"Think sourdough starter for a loaf of Amish friendship bread," answered Mama Effie.

"Exactly!" I said, amazed. "Wait, how do you know so much?"

Mama Effie, arched a brow and smiled. "Don't you worry about me. Just continue with your ranting, Boy. Get it all out."

"Giovanna sent the seed to Bear for safekeeping, but she didn't know he was dead and I was caught up in the middle of their messy catfight. Bishop, remember that goon's nose you ripped off back at the Odyssey Shop? Those are golems. Magically infused stone creatures that do your bidding. They were the very same kind of assassins the Lombardi sisters used on me as well as against each other.

"One of the golems gutted me like a fish and I downed the whole elixir in one gulp. Fixed me right up and gave me a completely clean slate. That's why I'm longer on your psychic party line, Simza." I pulled up my shirt and showed her my lean belly sans navel. "I don't even have fingerprints."

"Istenem…" Simza reached out to touch my stomach. I pulled away and tucked my shirt back in.

"Oh, that's just the tip of the crazy iceberg my world been in the past six months. I had my heart torn out, my head bashed in and my guts ripped out. One of the advantages of the Salt; it's damn hard to kill me.

"On the downside, I need to drink an infusion every hundred years or I'll turn to stone.

"I've seen a corpse come back to life and tear off a man's head like it was a bottle cap.

"I had a swamp monster grow from a shell I wore around my neck.

"By the way, I saw the Baskerville brothers in New Mexico. They were zombies that Harleaux had on a leash. I shot them both. I don't know what happened to Crabtree. I just hope he's dead. I mean, *really* dead.

"I was nearly eaten by fish people. Not beautiful mermaids, like in the fairytales. No, sir. These were insane, incestuous, shark faced, man eating fish people. The only thing that saved my skin was that the Salt in my blood turned their stomachs.

"And speaking of my blood, a cabal of 15th century alchemists has put a bounty on my head. Turns out that the stuff in my blood is the purest thing on the market. The tap they've been getting their Salt from isn't doing the trick anymore and they want to bleed me to save themselves from turning into planters.

"Still, to be fair, things were starting to look up after New Mexico. I got a lead to where my bastard brother stashed my gold and, thanks to the brilliant Giovanna Lombardi-Bonham, who had been a statue in my garden until my blood resurrected her-"

"So, that's what happened to it!" exclaimed Mama Effie. "I thought someone had stolen it."

"-created a Seed of the Salt of Life from the blood of Yours Truly. All I had to do was keep the Seed safe and let it grow for a hundred years and I'd be on Easy Street. For a brief second, I actually thought things were going good for me until *this* asshole shoved a gun in my face!"

I stood there, breathing heavily, wrung out and, quite frankly, unsure of everything I had just said. Had I just unloaded all my secrets?

My mother took it in stride. "If this horrible woman is dead, how did she get my amulet?"

"Harleaux possesses people, rides them. She doesn't have a body of her own. She was using her granddaughter, Pearl. Before that she was living inside her skull that her son kept in a bag hooked to his belt. Hell, I don't know how it works but that's how she gets around."

Bishop still wasn't on the bandwagon.

"Bullshit. All of this is bullshit. You should be writing for the radio, kid."

"I don't care if you believe me, Bishop. You can go to hell."

"Let's find Pearl then," said Simza. "Wherever she is, Harleaux must also be and where she is, I will find my amulet."

I shook my head. "She's dead. I buried her in New Mexico."

"Convenient." Bishop saluted me with a shot of whiskey. "Did she beg you, too?"

"I seem to have that effect on people." I remembered Pearl's eyes, crying for me to kill her and set her free. The white-hot flame I felt before unfurled inside my gut. "Want to try it out?"

"I've got nothing to do. Let's see you make me beg, boy."

He tossed back the whiskey and took a swing at me. I ducked and slammed an uppercut into his gut. He grunted, folded over, grabbed my wrist, and twisted me into a headlock. The rough fabric of his jacket felt like a cheese grater on my cheeks. I struggled to get free and he laughed, squeezing harder, until darkness started closing in.

"BOYS!" shouted Mama Effie. "Simza, did the amulet look like this?"

We both twisted around to see a sketch she'd drawn. Two circles. A Hand of Fatima on one and a circle with an X in the center on the other.

"Yes!" said Simza. "That is it."

"I've seen it," she said. "On the watch chain of Galante."

Bishop released me. "What does this mean?" he said.

"It's obvious." I said, rubbing my throat, feeling the blood rush back into my brain. "Harleaux is riding the Fat Man."

CHAPTER FOUR

Fight Fire with Fire

"Well," Mama Effie clapped her slender hands and smiled. "Now that we're all on the same page, I suggest we get the hell out of town."

"It's worse than you know," I said. "That man with the eyepatch? He's with the Order of Zosi-"

"Aaaaaaghhh!" Simza cried out and curled her left hand to her chest.

"What's wrong, sweetie?" Mama Effie put her arms around Simza's shoulders and held her. I think it was the only thing keeping my mother on her feet.

"He's near. I can feel it."

"How? How could he-"

I was cut off by the sounds of screams and terrified knocking on Mama Effie's chamber doors.

She opened the door and two women in silk sheath dresses ran in. Mama Effie closed the door behind them and locked it.

"What is it? What is happening?" she asked.

"We've been breached, ma'am," said a ginger haired girl. She had green eyes and an Irish lilt to her voice that I'm sure added extra spice to her going rate. "One fat bastard and a team of thugs just barreled through and started tearing the place down. Lulu rounded up the other girls and rushed them down to the tunnels."

"Christ!" said Bishop. "I thought you said this place was safe?"

"It is. Shut up." Mama Effie turned to the girls. "No one saw you come up here?"

"Veronica and me came up the back way." Ginger pointed to a raven-haired girl who clung behind her. "The boys in the band were tussling with them when we left but I don't think they stand much of a chance, ma'am."

"No matter." Mama Effie crossed over to her bedroom. She pulled on the frame of an oil painting of a woman bathing to reveal a secret door. Using the key Elliott had given her, she opened the door, unlocked the safe behind it, pulled out a doctor's bag, a ring of keys and handed them to Ginger. "Head down to the tunnels. When the coast is clear, take this bag to the bank manager, Mr. Tolliver. I've given the house over to you girls. Do with it what you will. Now, go!"

Gunshots rang out followed by heavy footsteps coming up the stairs and the girls left without another word.

"Guns! That's what we need," exclaimed Bishop. "You look like a girl who knows her business. You got some heat?"

"Plenty," said Mama Effie. "But I have something better."

"What?" I asked.

Mama Effie joined us in the sitting room, tapped three times on the wall beside the fireplace and the wall slid open to reveal a door on the other side.

"An escape route."

****

The door led to the townhouse next door. The wall slid shut and we stood in a boudoir, nice but not as elegant as the one we just left. A bed full of soft, plump pillows, satin drapes, and fresh flowers on the bed stand. The sheets in the bed were tossed to the side. Whoever had been here had left only moments before we came through the wall.

"You own both of these cathouses?" asked Bishop.

"I own the whole damn block, honey."

"Color me impressed." Bishop slicked back his hair with his hand. "I think I'm beginning to like you."

"Please, child," Mama Effie scoffed. "Your wallet isn't thick enough to make a deposit in my bank."

"You two can share a soda later," I said, breaking up their mating dance. "Can we get back on track? If you haven't forgotten, the only thing between us and a body hopping witch is one thin wall. Let's get moving!"

Just then, three knocks came from the other side of the wall.

"Helllloooooo." KNOCK. KNOCK. KNOCK. "Anyone home?"

Simza's dark eyes grew large and Mama Effie put a long finger to her lips. We all froze like statues, as if the very act of breathing would give us away.

"I know you're there, Jake." Harleaux said with Galante's lips. "Lover, don't let this suit scare you. It's only temporary. I'll find something prettier soon."

Bishop looked at me with disgust and mouthed the word, *WHAT?*

I shook my head and mouthed back, *IGNORE HER.*

Mama Effie rolled her eyes and pointed at the door, waving us towards it.

"Istenhegyi," Galante sang out in a strange falsetto a string of words of a language I did not know. The lights began to flicker and the air in the room began to smell like mold.

"AAARGH!" Simza fell to the floor a curled into a fetal position.

"Simza!" Mama Effie went to her friend's side and cradled her. "What is it, sweetie?"

Simza's mouth was opened in a silent scream and small tears of blood seeped from her eyes.

"What the hell is going on?" whispered Bishop.

"This has the stink of black magic on it," growled Mama Effie. She laid Simza down gently and stroked her head. "Not in my house, no sir. Not in MY house."

Mama Effie reached inside her blouse and plucked something out. It was dark purple and round, like an egg. She blew warm breath over it, said words in hushed tones and threw the egg to the floor. It shattered and a flood of spiders, tiny at first but grew bigger and bigger as they marched towards the wall. They crawled through the cracks and crevices and burrowed through into the other room.

Soon the shrieks of Harleaux battling the horde of spiders could be heard and the agony that wrapped itself Simza was broken. She took a deep breath and rolled onto her back. Whatever Mama Effie had done, it had broken the spell, if only for a moment.

"What the holy hell was that?" said Bishop.

"Fight fire with fire." She helped Simza up to her feet. "You won't last long in this game without learning few tricks, sugar."

"Oh, I like you more and more, lady!"

We followed her to a door that led even further down into tunnels where we met up with some of the ladies from the first house.

"What now?" I asked.

"Now? What do you think, boy?" Mama Effie looked at me as if I were thick as mud. "We get the hell out of New Orleans, that's what. I have some contacts, a few people in high places that owe me favors. I can get us even as far as Europe, if you're in the mood for a cruise."

"No way." I said. "I have to go back to the Odyssey Shop."

"Stupid child! Once I'm gone, I won't be able to protect you anymore. You understand that?"

Protect me? *Protect me?* These words are coming from a woman who made it a game to humiliate me, terrorize and goad me, day in and day out ever since I stepped foot into the Odyssey Shop to stake my claim as the new owner.

Then again, she had shielded me from the true business being done behind the façade of the Odyssey Shop so I could play Watson to Bear's erstwhile Sherlock Holmes. She tried to safeguard me when Dermot Brannigan wanted to take off my head. And what did that goon on the beach say right before he was eaten by fishpeople? *"Thank Mama Effie for saving your sweet ass this time."*

Maybe I had Mama Effie all wrong. Sure, she was mean, sarcastic and sometimes unnecessarily abusive but, under all that war paint and sequined polyester, she was covering my ignorant, stumbling ass. And never once did she ask for thanks.

I really was a stupid child.

"Thank you, Mama Effie but I'm not running away from this fight. It's time I stand firm. This ends here."

"Your funeral." Mama Effie shrugged her razor-sharp shoulders. "Simza, care to accompany me?"

"No," Simza shook her heard. "I am sorry but, no. The amulet. I must get it back."

Mama Effie smiled sadly and hugged her friend goodbye.

"How about you, cowboy?" Mama Effie turned to Bishop. "Fancy a luxury ride to Europe?"

Bishop bit his lip and rubbed his forehead in frustration. "Dammit all the hell but I go where he goes. I'm still on the clock and I'm not letting him slip through my fingers."

"Well, here's hoping you still have all ten when you get done." She winked. "Look me up sometime."

Bishop did something I didn't think he could do. He blushed.

"One more piece of business," she said and gave me a small silver key. "This opens the box where Bear's lease is kept, *Boss.*"

And with that cutting remark, Mama Effie, the most powerful, enraging, and terrifying woman I'd ever known, stepped into the busy streets of New Orleans and out of my life.

CHAPTER FIVE

Promises

Standing in a cold alleyway off Basin Street, my mother looked at me with wide open eyes, like a child. "Where now, Janos?"

Hell, I didn't have a clue.

I mentally checked off the few places I called home. The Odyssey Shop was a no go. That meant my apartment and all my earthly possessions were off the table. There was the Sun Coffee Shop where Bear and I were regulars but the last time I was there, I was on the run from thugs in fedoras. Not to mention the cannibal fish people.

Who could I turn to that might give me some shelter?

Only one name popped up: Frank Weiss. He was a retired journalist and old poker buddy of Bear's. He was always friendly to me but the last time I sought him out for help, things went bad. Like, broken bones and black eyes kind of bad. I really hoped he wouldn't hold that against me now.

He lived in an apartment above a bakery. We took the stairs up to his door. I knocked. The door open but only as far as the chain allowed. The dark eyes behind his glasses widened when he saw me.

"Go away, Jake. I told you never to come back."

"I thought you said this guy was a friend?" said Bishop.

"Who is that?" Frank strained to see who else was with me. "Who is she?"

"Hello, Frank. I'm Simza, Jake's mother. This is our friend, Mr. Bishop. May we come in?"

"Give us a break, buddy." added Bishop. "What kind of man leaves an old lady out in the cold?"

Simza smiled tightly and elbowed Bishop in the side. "Please?"

"Dammit." Frank closed the door, and I heard the swish of the chain as he unlocked the door. The door opened and he said, "Fine. But only because I'm a gentleman."

"Thank you, sir." Simza walked in first, followed by Bishop and then myself.

"I promise," I said to Frank. "We won't be any trouble."

Frank grunted as he closed the door. "We'll see about that."

His apartment was the same as I remembered. A single man's hovel. Towers of books, magazines and newspapers. A living room with a couch and a card table with four chairs that doubled for dining and poker games. A bedroom that held a single bed and a chifforobe. A bathroom that also doubled as his darkroom. A small kitchen where beans and potatoes were the main fare most days. The thick yeasty smell from the bakery downstairs clouded the room with a fake sense of domesticity.

I wish I could say that Frank looked the same. He was still wearing the same old brown cardigan but the sprightly gnome I remembered was gone. There was a weariness and fear in his face that I knew was partly my fault. Scratch that. It was all my fault. It was because of me that Dermot Brannigan sicced his boys on Frank, broke his arm and blackened his eye.

"Sit where you like," Fred said as he pulled a chair from the card table and sat with his back against the wall.

We all three sat awkwardly on the couch.

"Are you baking something, Frank?" Simza asked. "It smells delicious."

"What? No, that's the bakery downstairs. I can't smell much anymore." He tapped the side of his nose. "Darkroom chemicals burned out my sniffer. I suspect that's what you're here for, Jake? Need to use Ol' Fred for his darkroom again?"

"Not this time. I..we..um…we were in the neighborhood and, um…"

My lips flapped as my mind went blank. I didn't know what to say. How do you tell the person who suffered a broken bone the last time you spoke that you were on the run and needed a place to hide out until you figured what to do next?

"Thought we'd pop in for a visit," I said.

The words landed on the floor with a thud.

"A visit?" Frank Weiss' stare felt like a sledgehammer in my gut. "Do you think I'm a fool, son?"

"I think it's time for us to go," said Bishop. "I don't like this guy's attitude."

"Go where? Where are you going to go? Back to the Odyssey Shop?" Frank snorted. "You think I don't know something hinkey is going on over there? That I don't have contacts? Twenty years as a reporter on the crime beat and I don't know when dirt is being kicked up? I got people telling me that the Odyssey Shop is under new management. That the new bosses are cutting ties with all the games in town and that is making a lot of people in the underground very unhappy. And the name that everybody keeps saying, over and over again is Jake Istenhegyi.

"You're here because you don't have anywhere else *to* go. That's the only reason you'd show up on my doorstep. So, quit yanking my chain and tell me what's going on."

So, I told him. A very bare bones version, of course, where I came home from a business trip and get bushwhacked by thugs. I didn't see a reason to include body switching witches, golems, or immortal elixirs.

Frank rubbed his chin. "And you think they want to squeeze you out of your share of the property?"

Or every drop of blood out of me. I nodded. "Something like that."

"What about Bear? My people can't get a lead on him."

"He's lying low."

"On sabbatical," said Bishop. "So I hear."

"Uh-huh. He does that a lot lately. And who are these two? How do they fit in?"

"This is Raymond Bishop, a private detective from Los Angeles," I said.

"An old friend of Bear's." Bishop chimed in. "Looking to reconnect."

"And this is your mother?" asked Frank.

"Also in town to reconnect," she said. "Who knew my son lived such an interesting life?"

The lies comforted Frank and he relaxed in his chair.

"So, how can I help?" he asked.

"We need somewhere off their grid to rest and recoup."

"Some hot grub wouldn't be refused," said Bishop.

"A safe place, out of the cold, to arrrgh!" Simza gasped and clenched her left hand into a fist.

"What's wrong?" said Frank. "Is she having a heart attack?"

"They are near, Janos." She opened her fist and the spidery veins that lined her palm pulsated and spread another half inch.

"How did they find us?" asked Bishop.

"It's my fault, I'm afraid." Simza said. "The amulet. They must be tracking us through it."

There was a heavy knock at the door.

Frank stared at us with eyes as wide as soup bowls.

"Don't answer that," said Bishop.

The knocking grew louder, shaking the door frame.

"Who is it?" called out Frank.

Silence.

"No solicitors, thank you." Frank continued. "Go away."

And then another KNOCK! And the door caved in.

Two Valentinoesque golems strode in.

"I said, No Solicitors!"

Frank pulled a Winchester 1897 shotgun that he had taped under the card table, pumped it once and fired, hitting one golem in the head and knocking another backwards like dominoes.

"What the hell, Frank?" I asked.

"I didn't like being a victim. So, I got a gun."

He cocked the shotgun again, ran to the door and fired a shot. "I've got three more shells and then we're up shit creek. Any ideas?"

"Is there another way out of here?" I asked.

Frank shook his head.

"Do you see a fat son of a bitch out there?" asked Bishop.

"Yeah."

"Shoot him!"

"No!" I yelled. "Wait!

Frank cocked the barrel and shot. There was a low, guttural cry and a thud.

"Got him. Now what?"

The ground began to shake, lights flickered and a cold wind roared through the apartment. The towers of books and magazines toppled over at my feet. I looked down and saw a *Black Mask* magazine. One of Bears? Maybe he had left it behind after one of their all-night poker games. I grabbed it and tucked it into my jacket pocket.

"What the hell?" said Bishop.

"This isn't good," I murmured.

The wind circled around Frank Weiss, picking him up and tossing him around like a rag doll. He screamed, long and hollow. It was as if he was being pulled inside out. His body arced impossibly backwards, as if he were struck by lightning, and then straightened out, his arms and legs stretched out like a X. Our eyes met for a brief second until his head jerked to the right and snapped. There was another rumble, shaking the room like a train was running through it and then silence. His body hung in the air for a terrible second and then fell. His arms and legs were splayed out like an unstrung marionette. His neck looked unnaturally long as his head laid on his right shoulder. His eyes were open and clear. The gray cataract that comes with death had not settled in yet.

"Oh, that poor man." Simza moved towards him to help but I stopped her.

"Is he dead?" asked Bishop.

A low moan escaped from Frank's mouth.

"He lives, Janos. I can help him," she said.

"Wait," I replied.

His head shuddered and did a rickety click-click-click motion, like a car on a rollercoaster making its way up a hill. The skull lined up on the spine, the head turned to the left, CLICK! and then to the right, CLICK! His head lolled around in a circle, as if testing the new joints. Once in place, Frank sat up, his arms dangling as if unhinged. He rolled his shoulders as if he were trying out the fit of a new jacket. A long, satisfied breath escaped his lips as he stood up, gripped the shotgun and turned the barrel towards us.

"Oh, lover," he said, smiling. "You screwed up good now."

CHAPTER SIX

Open a Vein

"Nice going, Bishop. Good job."

"Well, I didn't know," Bishop huffed and growled under his breath, "That's Harleaux? Inside Frank?"

I nodded.

"Christ."

"You didn't have to kill Frank, you bitch."

"I'm afraid I do, sweetie. I can only ride family. Blood connects blood. Anyone else, well," Harleaux shrugged. "Corpses aren't the most pleasant accommodations, but one does what one must."

"It's okay. We got this," said Bishop. "There are only two shots left and there are three of us. We can take him, er, her. What the hell do I call it?"

"My name," she said, pointed the barrel at Simza and pulled the trigger. She screamed as the shell slammed into her leg, shattering her thigh bone. "Is Henrietta Harleaux. And now I only have one shell left." Harleaux cocked the shotgun. "Who wants it?"

"You bastard!" I scrambled to grab my mother as she fell.

"What the hell! Jesus!" Bishop shouted as he knelt down, whipped off his belt and used it as a tourniquet on her leg. She grimaced as Bishop pulled it tighter. Her breathing was fast as her eyes rolled back and she passed out.

"Christ! Is she dead?"

"Not yet," said Bishop.

"You bitch!" I leapt up and stood in front of the gun barrel. "I'll take you on. Right here and now!"

"That would be a waste of a bullet, sweetheart. As I've had the misfortune to learn, you are a hard man to kill." Harleaux took a step the side. "I could use my last shell on him, right in the head. They only want you, lover."

"No!"

"Or we skip all this brouhaha and get your sweet ass back to the Odyssey Shop."

"Impossible. We need an ambulance. She can't be moved," said Bishop.

"Then I guess she dies here or..." Harleaux's face took on a sick, feral sheen. "I've heard some amazing stories about that blood of yours, Istenhegyi. Let's experiment. Open a vein. Let's see what happens."

"Jesus...you're insane," I said.

Bishop looked desperate. "She's going to die if we don't do something."

Simza was unconscious but I knew what she'd say.

"Leave me, Janos…save yourself."

Or that's what I'd like to think she'd say.

"Dammit."

I found a knife in Frank's kitchen, cut my hand, and let the blood pool in the center of my right palm.

Harleaux bit her lip in excitement.

"I can't promise this will work," I said.

Bishop shrugged. "Kid, she doesn't have anything else."

I knelt and slapped my hand over the hole in her thigh.

Two things happened very quickly.

The moment my blood touched her skin, my mother moaned and her back arched like electricity was shooting out from my hands. Her head rocked back and forth and her long dark hair flailed around like tentacles.

Then the lightening boomeranged, slamming me across the room. I heard Bishop calling my name, his voice becoming fainter and fainter as I fell further and further away. My breath rushed out of my lungs as my body hit the hardwood floor-

But I kept falling.

Images, as if someone were thumbing through a photo album, flipped past me.

Trees, campfires, city streets, a stone mansion that I recognized as my grandmother's home, a place I spent most of my childhood before I was shuttled away to boarding school, my father, young, smiling, carefree, almost unrecognizable. In his arms was Simza. She turned towards me, her face glowing with that look of fresh, new love. She reached out to me, my mother, and caressed my face. Sparks tickled my cheeks as she touched me, looking at me intensely, as if trying to engrave my profile into her brain like a photograph.

"My Janos. I missed you so much..." The words weren't spoken. No language was needed. I could feel her love and desperate longing.

Around us a swirled a storm of colors, blue, red and purple. The colors solidified into three cords, reared back like cobras and slammed into me, spearing through my skin and pouring into my veins. I was the center of everything. Absolutely all things were within my grasp. I was filled. No part of me ached or needed for anything.

Suddenly, lines of thick black oil cracked through the storm. The colors dimmed and rolled back like wilting leaves. The poison reared back like a snake, coiled and writhing, it twisted like taffy and whipped itself at me. I lunged back, out of its strike zone. It struck out again and hit home, black, sharp fangs stabbing into my neck. The pain tore into me and I tried to scream but nothing would come out. I knew instinctively that this was somehow because of Harleaux. The longer the bitch had the coin, the more my mother would be poisoned and all this power, this raw, beautiful storm of color would die or worse.

Suddenly, the snake convulsed and pulled out of my neck. It hung over me, dripping black ink until it disappeared as if pulled backwards by an invisible rope.

Minutes, seconds, hours fell away until a rough slap stung my cheek. The pain rang my bell and brought me gasping back to cold reality. I opened my eyes to see Harleaux standing over me with a pair of golems by her side.

I sat up to see that, on the other side of the room, the situation had been reversed. Bishop was being nursed my Simza. On his forehead a purple goose egg was started to sprout.

"Simza, did it work?"

She nodded and returned to caring for Bishop.

"Bishop, what the hell happened to you?"

"After you hit the floor, Frank...Harleaux, whatever that thing is, collapsed. Hit the floor like a bag of potatoes. I saw my chance to get the gun but one of those damn stone goons got to me first."

Harleaux squatted beside me with a feline grace that I doubt the old man had ever possessed. She stared at me. No, that's wrong. She stared *into* me. Frank's soft brown eyes turning onyx black as her head swayed like a cobra trying to entrance a mongoose.

"What are you Jake Istenhegyi?" she hissed. The smell on her breath made me gag.

"I'm nothing," I said. "I'm just a stupid son of a bitch that tripped down a rabbit hole and has been scrambling to find his way out ever since."

She unfolded from her crouch, unnaturally graceful, her cold stony stare never breaking. "Oh, lover, you are *something*. And so is she." The tongue slithered out from between the lips like a snake tasting the air. "And I think it's time we made our way back to the Odyssey Shop to find out what."

Enjoying the Ride

The golems cleaned up their fallen brethren and threw their crumbled pieces into the back of a pickup truck. Bishop and Simza had their hands tied behind their backs and were hustled away in an ordinary gray Ford Packard.

I was left unhindered. It was more of a blow to my ego than you'd think. Harleaux knew she had me. Why waste the rope?

The car waiting for us was a two toned red and black, Grosser Mercedes Pullman limousine with a driver decked out in livery. The inside was decked out like a luxury train car. A stocked bar with a cut crystal decanter, a privacy screen, facing leather seats, and a thick braided golden rope to signal the driver in front when our ice got too warm. The only fault I could find was the lack of leg room because the body of Onofrio Galante was lying on the floorboard between us.

"I hope you don't mind sharing. They didn't have room in the Packard. Oh, and before I forget." Harleaux reached down and rummaged in the dead man's pockets.

"Ah, here we are." She pulled out a vial with a cork top. "I'd hate to lose this."

A flash of the obvious went off inside my head. "That's you tracked us. My blood. The samples stolen from Giovanna's lab."

"Clever boy." Harleaux put her feet on the corpse and stretched out, balancing the shotgun on her lap. The corpse of the fat man jiggled, causing the amulet to slip out and dangle on the end of the keychain. I felt like a cat being teased with a bell. Strangely, Harleaux didn't seem to notice it at all. It occurred to me then that she had no idea about its power. She probably found it in my jacket and kept it as a trophy, a reminder of leaving me behind in the swamp. Relief flooded through me. That was at least one thing in my favor.

"What are you smiling about?" she said.

"Nothing. Just enjoying the ride," I said. "Enough small talk. What do you want from me, Harleaux? What are you getting out of this?"

"What do I want? I thought it would be obvious by now. I want what you took from me." She let out a long hiss and her head cocked unnaturally to one side and leaned forward, her chest incredibly inflating like a cobra's hood. "You ruined my life, Istenhegyi."

"Me? That's not how I remember it. You were murdering people."

"I was providing for my family."

"You killed my best friend."

"*You killed me!* You burned down my temple, destroyed my loas, and consigned me to this, *this!*" She pulled at the thin wisps of hair on the old man's head. "I can feel this body rotting all around me. You could have left me inside my skull but no. You stole it and tossed it to that infernal swamp monster."

Ah, yes. The Boodaddy. The elemental creature that grew from a talisman Wayburn Crabtree gave me for protection from the legendary Honey Island Swamp Monster. We had gone out there looking for pirate treasure only to find that it was all a ruse put on by Harleaux to kill me. I pulled a fast one and hurled her skull, two fingers in each bony eye socket, like a bowling ball, into the swamp. The Boodaddy caught it midair with its veiny kudzu tendrils, buried it deep inside itself and vanished into the swamp. I smiled at the memory.

"It's good to have friends in swampy places."

"Don't get cocky, boy. The Order has promised to make me whole." She sneered in disgust as she looked at her liver spotted hands. "I won't need *this*."

"And then what?"

"Go home. I have family that will beg to host me." She leaned in close and I could smell the lingering smell of baked bread on the old man's sweater and stale breath from his cooling, dead mouth. "Most importantly, Pearl's baby boy is all alone. Motherless. Every boy needs a mother, don't you think?"

CHAPTER EIGHT

Odyssey Shop

The car slowed to a stop outside the Odyssey Shop.

Harleaux opened the car door to a phalanx of Valentinos lined up from the sidewalk to the building. They stood shoulder to shoulder. I doubt I could've slid a quarter between them. It delivered an obvious message that there was no way to escape.

I kept remembering Giovanna's warning, *"Jake, if they find you, they will strap you to a board, jam needles permanently into your veins and milk you, bringing you to the point of death, waiting until you recover before they start the process over and over again until they have a workable crystal synthesized from the Salt in your blood."*

Jesus, is this how it ends? Hooked up like a cow and suckled on by greedy old men desperate to keep on living?

Sunlight glinted off Simza's amulet on Galante's chain. I knew then that if this was going to end on a high note, I had to do it now.

"Welcome home, Jake Istenhegyi," she said and stepped out of the car. "Time to go."

"Okay, don't push me," I said and then stumbled, catching myself with my left hand on the corpse. With my right hand, I grabbed the coin and yanked it off the chain. "Sorry, legs fell asleep," I said scrambling out of the car and palming the coin into my front pants pocket.

With my mother's amulet in my pocket, a cloud lifted off my shoulders. If I never saw sunlight again, at least Simza would be free from Harleaux.

I took a step forward and the golems closed in behind me, like a zipper, forcing me to go forward. I twisted to see Harleaux but I couldn't see her beyond the Valentinos.

The front door of the Odyssey Shop slowly opened.

"Mr. Istenhegyi, I presume?"

In the doorway stood a very athletic, young man in a suit tailor cut to cover his muscles. He crossed his arms and said with a casual, friendly tone. "You've been a difficult man to find."

"You're not the first one to say that to me lately."

"I'm Jeffrey Crow, head of security. Mr. Barone is looking forward to meeting you but, first, I need to check you for weapons."

"I don't have anything."

"Just a precaution. Please. Put your hands up."

I put my hands on my head as he patted me down.

He pulled the Black Mask magazine out from my jacket and looked at me smugly.

"What? I like to read. Sue me."

He shoved it back in my jacket. His hands reached my waist, ran a finger around my belt line and then patted down each leg. Our eyes met when he felt my pocket.

The coin in my pocket suddenly felt like a brick. If he tried to take it, what would I do? I calculated the odds of how far I'd get if I punched him. That's depending, of course, that he was human. If I punched a golem in the face, all I'd get is a broken hand for my troubles.

"Oh, stop it, Jeffrey, that's not necessary. Not necessary at all!" The voice was high and reedy but strong.

Jeffrey stepped away and addressed the old man in the wheelchair. "Mr. Barone, there are protocols. You hired me to protect you."

The old man's wheelchair took up the entire doorway. It was as monstrous as Mama Effie described it. A wheezing iron lung on wheels with two tubes that looped up from behind and nested into two apertures in the chest right above what looked like a family crest. It was a knotted ball stabbed through by a sword.

None of it explained the man sitting in the chair.

Mama Effie described him as a sickly stick man but that wasn't what I saw. He wouldn't be competing in the Olympics but the parts of the man exposed, his upper chest, neck and head, were of a man in the bloom of health. Well, as much as an elderly man of 500 years could blossom.

I will concede that Mama Effie was right about one thing: the chair leaked.

And I wouldn't bet the farm that the rusty, brown spots that trailed behind it weren't blood.

Barone shooed the young man away as a golem pushed the chair towards me.

"Mr. Istenhegyi is my business partner, not a criminal, not a thief, and definitely not an assassin. I am a fine judge of character, young man. You don't get to my age without knowing prey from predator. Are you armed, Mr. Istenhegyi?"

I shook my head.

"Of course, you aren't. Now, step aside, Jeffrey and let's go back inside. My blood is too thin for this cold."

"As you will, sir," said Jeffrey.

The golem rolled the old man's wheezing wheelchair back inside and I followed dutifully behind.

And that's how I entered the Odyssey Shop for the final time.

CHAPTER NINE

A Strange Home Sickness

A wave of vertigo hit me as soon as I crossed the threshold. A strange home sickness hit me, but I wasn't going to let it show.

First of all, let's get one fact straight. The Odyssey Shop was a rathole, but it was *my* rathole. A place I'd called home for five years.

The room I walked into was not the Odyssey Shop I knew.

The filthy, unwelcoming facade of the storefront had been transformed into a European salon. Mama Effie's desk and register, the throne where she ruled over her crooked fiefdom was removed and replaced with a Persian rug, mahogany coffee table with a marble top and slender legs and elegant couch and love seats that looked like something the Sun King would've rested his royal derriere.

"Welcome home, Mr. Istenhegyi," said Barone. "I had Cook prepare something for you to eat."

"Later." I said. "Where are the man and woman that were brought here before me?"

"They are upstairs, in your apartment."

"I hope nothing of mine has been tampered with?"

"The floor above has remained unchanged." Barone motioned with his head at his wheelchair. "I prefer to keep myself grounded."

"Good. Stay that way." I rushed up the stairs. Jeffrey the bodyguard broke away and followed me.

The door to my apartment was closed. I knocked.

Bishop cracked the door open, saw my face and opened wide.

"Jake! Where the hell have you been?"

"Janos?" My mother's worried voice cut in behind Bishop's. "Slava Domnului!" *Thank God.*

"Don't start thanking God quite yet," I said. Jeffrey followed closely behind as I entered. "We're still in the lion's den."

My apartment was just as I had left it. Spartan, except for the essentials: a bed, a toilet and a hot plate. Pretty much all I need. A life of constant travel never really taught me how to be domestic.

Simza threw her arms around me and hugged me tightly. "I was so afraid for you, Janos. That man downstairs. He smells of death. I do not trust him."

"That's a good call." I gave her a quick hug, hard enough so she'd let go. "Are you both all right?"

"Except for the fact this asshole won't let us leave," said Bishop, jutting a jaw towards Jeffrey. "Everything's peaches and cream."

A man with the face of a boxer and fists like boulders knocked on the door. "Hey, Boss. We got a problem. Need you fast."

Jeffrey sighed. "David, stand guard outside the door and escort Istenhegyi to Mr. Barone in five minutes."

Bishop closed the door after Jeffrey left.

"What's going on, Jake? What's the plan?"

"Plan? A day ago, you thought I was a murderer. You have a lot of confidence in me if you suddenly think I have a plan."

"Beautiful." Bishop rubbed his face and sat down on the bed. "We just sit here and wait? For what? A miracle?"

"It's always worked before," I said. "Simza, I need to talk to you."

I took her by the arm, and we stood by the window that overlooked the back alley.

"What is it, Janos?"

"I have something for you." I held up the coin. "Voila!"

"Janos, that is wonderful! Where did you find it?"

I grimaced at the memory of plucking it off a corpse.

"Don't ask. Just be happy to have it back."

I held it out, but she shook her head. She folded my fingers around it, pressing it into my palm.

"It is yours, my son."

"Don't you need it?"

"No." She put her palm down over mine and I felt heat pressing down into my hand. There was a tingling that resonated up my arm and through my fingertips. "A mother always protects her child.

"See?" She held up her palm. The black lines were slowly shrinking. "The darkness is already receding."

Bishop coughed. "Pardon but I need to take a shower. Does it work, Jake?"

I slid the coin into my pocket and nodded. "One of the few things that does in this old building."

"And I need to rest." Sizma kissed my cheek. "Go and see to your friend. He needs you."

"Barone can wait," I said.

"I'm not talking about him."

CHAPTER TEN

Null and Void

David the Thug stopped me outside my door.

"Where do you think you're going?"

"Need to take a piss."

"Why don't you use the one in there?"

"Bishop's taking a shower, so I figured I'd use the toilet in Bear's office. I hope you don't want to hold my hand because I kind of need both."

David grimaced, shook his head, and pushed me forward.

I went downstairs and closed the door behind me.

The room was dark. Sunlight cutting through the blinds was the only source of light.

Barrington Gunn, a survivor of Gallipoli but now a very dead private detective, sat at his desk, staring glumly at the bourbon in front of him. He reached out to grab the bottle, but his fingers passed through the neck like smoke. He did this motion, over and over. He never blinked, just kept reaching and grabbing, his fingers forever disappearing into the slender brown bottle neck.

I pulled up a chair, the same one I always sat in during our detective days. Back then, he'd sit behind the desk with his gigantic feet up and leaning so far back as to make the chair groan in pain. I'd sit patiently in my space, waiting for orders.

"Bear?"

I said his name three more times before he slowly looked up at me. It took another heartbeat for him to focus on me.

"Jake?" It was as if a connection was made and a light came on behind his eyes. "Jake!"

But the light flared and dimmed.

"Jake, where am I?"

"You're in your office. Looks like you're trying to get a drink. Mind if I join you?"

I took his silence for consent and went around to his side of the desk, pulled open a drawer and fished out two glasses. Then something else caught my eye. A locked metal container, the size of a cigar box. There were squiggly marks carved into the top that hurt my eyes if I looked at it for too long. They moved and squirmed like metal worms.

"What's in the box?"

"I don't remember. Something important." He sounded groggy, like a child woken from his nap too early. "Fireproof. Mama Effie told me to keep it safe. Contracts."

I removed the locked box. Bear didn't react. I sat down in my chair and poured amber gold in the glasses. I took a drink and tried not to cough as it burned down my throat.

"Jesus, Bear! You never had any taste for the finer things, did you?"

He flickered. A quick moment of being and nothing. He was dwindling, unraveling, a filament burning itself through until the bulb was empty glass.

I didn't have much time.

"Did you hear about the new management?" I said as I fished out the key Mama Effie had given me from my pocket. "Boy, did they do a number downstairs. It looks like goddamn Versailles. You'd hate it, Bear."

The worms stopped wriggling once I turned the key and opened the box. Inside, was a rolled-up scroll tied shut with a ruddy brown cord that looked like dried tripe. I didn't even want to guess what kind of animal they used. Or if it was animal.

I removed the scroll. The lease Bear had signed years ago. The contract that kept him bound to the Odyssey Shop. Christ, it was warm. I broke the cord, unfurled the parchment, and read it. Yeah, this was it.

I rolled the scroll back up.

"This new guy, Mr. Barone, I don't know what to make of him yet. Gives me the heebie jeebies. I wish I could get your bead on the guy. You were always good at that." My throat felt tight. "I don't know what those bozos want to do with the Odyssey Shop, but I do know one thing: I am still the *boss*. What I say *goes*."

Bear's eyes brightened, and he snorted out a gruff laugh. "Settle down, Bela."

"For the last time, I do not sound like Bela Lugosi. You son of a bitch."

I held up his lease.

"Barrington Gunn, I, Janos Istenhegyi, the rightful owner of this establishment, release you from any and all signed contracts between you and the entity known as the Odyssey Shop."

I gripped the scroll with both hands and twisted. There was resistance, as if it were made of something sturdier than parchment.

"Son of a bitch! You will obey me!" I stood, kicking the chair behind me. "As the owner of this establishment, as the goddamn BOSS, I declare this contract NULL AND VOID!"

I gritted my teeth and growled in sadness and anger as it finally ripped in two. Sparks leapt and snapped my fingertips and the air filled with the smell of ozone and spice.

The chair in front of me was empty.

And so was Bear's glass of bourbon.

For some stupid, crazy reason that empty glass made it all right.

I took the folded Black Mask magazine out of my jacket pocket and laid it on his desk.

"Goodbye, Bear."

CHAPTER ELEVEN

Alone

David the thug was waiting patiently in the hall.

I didn't say anything to him as I walked past him. I'd just sent my best friend to the Great Beyond. I wasn't in the mood for chit chat.

He followed right behind me, step for step as I went down to face Barone.

I've never felt more alone in my life.

King's Favorite Cow

Vincenzo Barone's hideous wheelchair was parked beside the dining table. There was a small dark pool underneath it.

"Come, sit down. Eat," he said. "I have found it is always best to do business over food. It is the mark of a civilized man."

I don't remember sitting down at the table as much as my stomach pulling me towards it. I had not eaten in over a day and the rumbling in my belly was all the reminding I needed.

An elderly white man in a white apron with a tall chef's hat rolled out a marble butler's table. On it was a large bowl made of what looked like onyx with matching ladle. Two young women, possibly children by their sizes, swiftly appeared to each side of me, putting down a plate, a bowl, silverware, a linen napkin in my lap, two crystal glasses, one for wine the other for water, as if by magic. The chef served the stew, put a bowl of warm bread out for me and just as quickly disappeared. The smell of the food made my mouth water and my stomach growl. I started to dig in but then I noticed that Vincenzo Barone had no food in front of him.

"Are you not eating?" I asked.

"No. Unfortunately, I am unable to enjoy such luxuries but, please, let me enjoy your pleasure as you eat."

I dropped the spoon. "I just lost my appetite."

A light went on inside Barone's pale brown eyes and he laughed. "Dear boy, that is precious. What would I gain to taint the well? Besides, how long would any poison affect you?"

"Long enough for you to strap me down to a table and start milking me for blood."

"Good Lord, where would you get such ghoulish ideas? Honestly."

"Giovanna Lombardi warned me what you had planned."

"Oh. And how could she possibly divine what the Order had planned? Unless, of course, it was because it was something she herself would do, if the circumstances were reversed?"

His words struck a nerve. When Giovanna had told me what she feared the Order wanted to do to me, I said, jokingly, how did she know. She replied, *"I know because it was what I would have done, once upon a time."*

"I understand Onofrio met with an unfortunate accident," said Barone. "I gather our Miss Harleaux has found new accommodations?"

I nodded. "She killed a friend of mine. I'm not very happy about that. I haven't seen her since we got back to the Shop. She disappeared in the crowd."

"Unpleasant. Unfortunate. Que sera, sera. Between us, I'll be happy to be rid of her. She's unfinished business, a reminder of the old Order. I'd love to clear the ledger of the entire business."

"I hope she doesn't hear you say that."

I tore the bread in halves and used them to sponge up the stew as Barone waxed on, trying to serenade me. To be honest, I only heard one of every three words, until he said: "I own you."

"Excuse me?"

"When the Order bought the Odyssey Shop, it also took on the accounts of any debtors." Barone's eyes never flinched. "In buying this dilapidated piece of real estate, for pennies on the dollar, I want to add, we acquired you, our primary objective. Banking can be so exhilarating, don't you think?"

"And there goes my appetite."

"You misunderstand me, my dear boy. While I humbly admit that the Order of Zosimos does not have lily white hands, I can tell you this much," Vincenzo Barone leaned his head toward me and winked. "That was the old Order. The slate is wiped clean and a new Order is at hand."

"What does that mean?"

"I want you as a partner. Mr. Istenhegyi, I can give you the world. You will never want for anything. You can walk away from this hellhole and start a whole new life."

"And all you want from me is access to what's flowing in my veins?"

"It's a fair deal. You will benefit as much as I will. Trust me. A century flies by faster than you think. Oh, and, best of all," he continued. "I want to bring Miss Giovanna Lombardi-Bonham into the fold. I need to a mind as brilliant as hers to restart my research facility. She will have the most up to date facilities to work in and all the freedom and time to do it in."

"It'll be a hard sell," I said. "She's not a fan of the Order."

Barone made a garbled laugh. "See the symbol on my chest?" he said. "It's my family crest. The Gordian Knot undone with the tip of a sword. *A Simplex Via.* The simpler way. It is my code. It is the reason why the Order failed. Those old fools forgot what we were, in the beginning."

"And what's that?"

"We are bankers. There are profits and losses, a ledger to keep balanced. We provided the capital and the partners did all the muck work. All that alchemy, dabbling in dark sciences. It's best to leave that sort of work to experts, to minds like Lombardi and the like. She has assets we can utilize and monopolize. Far better than all this running around the world, wasting resources, kidnapping, using assassins. Pffft." Barone shook his head. "There's nothing that can be done with a sword that can't be done quicker and easier with a pen and a contract."

I did a quick bit of accounting for myself. Thirteen chairs. Thirteen members. Mama Effie said she saw twelve sarcophagi on the stage in the storage room.

"Where are they now?" I motioned to the empty chairs. "The rest of the bankers?"

"They liquidized their assets and disbanded from the company."

The sound of clapping caught my attention. It was Lucio Amara. Or I should say what was left of the Lucio. What walked towards me was a husk, dried out and wheezing. A plastic tube the diameter of my fist punched the side of his neck and trailed over his shoulder. The empty hole that he had covered with an eyepatch was weeping gray white ash. With every breath, the veins in his face would pulsate as if straining to push the blood through his body as he walked towards the dining room table, slowly clapping his hands.

"Liquidized," said Amara. "You always had a silver tongue, you slick bastard."

Barone's face was scarlet with fury. "JEFFREY!"

Lucio pulled out a chair next to me and gestured, *May I?*

"Good evening, Lucio." I kept my face placid even though my stomach wanted to revolt. "I wondered if you were sulking around."

"Lamb?" He dipped a skeletal finger in the stew, snagged a tasty morsel and put it up to his lips and smiled. "They offered me lamb for my first meal. Remember, Vincenzo? The night the Order of Zosimos pulled me out of the fire?"

Jeffrey burst through the front door, winded and confused. "Sir, we've got a situation. There's a body...oh, hell."

"Oh hell, indeed! How did he get out of...?" Angry spittle bubbled at the corner of Barone's mouth.

"The sarcophagi under the stage in the utility room?" I said.

All three men looked at me in shock.

"I might not have the entire puzzle," I said, "but I do have a lot of the pieces."

Lucio cackled as he dipped his finger into my stew again. He leaned closer, sprinkling ash from his eyehole in the stew. "Let me fill in the empty spaces.

"I was an easy target. I didn't have anything when they took me in. I was a thief. No home, no family. The Order offered me everything and all they asked in return was a small donation: a pint for each member. And for centuries, I lived like a king. Well, to be honest, like the king's favorite cow.

"And do you know what happens to cows that stop producing milk?"

"Jeffrey!" Barone screeched. I imagined that the body inside that rolling iron lung was shaking with frustration. "For God's sake, do your duty! Remove him!"

"Let's not make scene." Jeffrey slapped a hand on Lucio's shoulder and stumbled forward as the bone crumbled away and his arm fell to the floor in a dusty heap.

"Holy shit!" Jeffrey shouted and did a two-step to keep from falling on his face.

Lucio looked down at his arm and then back up at me. He was grinning.

"It doesn't hurt, in case you're wondering," he said. "But take a long hard look, Jake Istenhegyi. In the end, *this* is what that bastard is offering you."

Just then, Bishop, naked but for only a towel wrapped around his waist, burst into the dining room.

"Jake! Something's wrong with Simza....*what the hell is that?*"

Amara waved hello with his remaining hand.

"Never mind. What happened to Simza?"

"I came out of the shower and she was having another seizure like before at Frank's house," he explained. "I held her down to keep her from hurting herself and then she just went limp. I can't wake her up."

"I'll go get my medical bag," said Jeffrey. "I'm a...I was a doctor."

"You all go ahead," said Lucio, sitting in my place and tucking the napkin under his chin. Barone fumed by his side. "I'll finish up your stew. Vinnie and I can talk over old times."

CHAPTER THIRTEEN

A Matter of Privacy

Simza lied motionless on the bed.

I touched her cheeks. They were cold. She wasn't breathing.

"Simza!" I shook her, gently slapping her cheeks as I tried to wake her up. I felt helpless, not knowing what else to do.

Jeffrey ran in and pulled me away. "I got this." He opened up a black doctor's bag, retrieved a small tin. He opened it and pulled out what looked like a pinky sized tube wrapped in a white cotton bandage. He snapped it between his fingers and waved it under her nose. The smell of ammonia burned my nose.

Simza gasped and opened her eyes. "What are you doing? Get off me!"

A welcomed wave of relief washed over me as she pushed Jeffrey. She was angry. Angry is good. Angry is alive.

"You're okay?" I asked.

She stood up, a bit wobbly but smiling. "The darkness," she said. "She came back. We fought." She held up her palm. It was clear of any blemish. "I won."

"Jesus, more hoodoo bullshit." Bishop shook his head. "I'm gonna go get dressed. I'm freezing my balls off." He left us and closed the pocket doors that separated the bedroom from the living area.

"Let me examine you anyway." Jeffrey reached for his stethoscope. "Best to be sure."

"No!" she said, slapping away his hand.

"Just let him check your heart, Simza,' I said.

"I'm fine. Just let me be!" She opened the pocket doors and we heard Bishop yell, "Hey, how about some damn privacy, lady!" as the doors slammed shut.

Jeffrey folded his stethoscope and put it back in his back. "I'm glad to see that she is well. Last thing we need around here is another body."

"What do you mean?" I asked.

"Found an old guy out in the alleyway. Mr. Barone isn't going to like it, but I had to call the police. The meat wagon is on the way."

The warm feeling of relief I had quickly chilled.

"Show me the body."

CHAPTER FOURTEEN

The Favor

A few moments later, Jeffrey took me to the alleyway behind the Odyssey Shop.

I stood over the discarded body of Frank Weiss and a tsunami of emotions crashed into my chest: grief, guilt and, not least of all, anger.

But I didn't have time to mourn.

"You know this guy?" said Jeffrey. "I figured he was just a drunk. Maybe he got rolled by some other vagrants. We get all kinds around here."

I turned my attention back to the building, looked up and saw Simza standing at the window, staring down at us.

Our eyes met and she smiled.

"That *bitch*," I growled and ran towards the Shop, Jeffrey barely keeping up as rage fueled every footstep.

We didn't get very far before two of my old friends, the Stone Valentinos, showed up. One tried to clothesline me. I dodged but Jeffrey wasn't quite so nimble. He was knocked down on his ass. The second golem closed rank and grabbed me by the throat and lifted me off my feet. I kicked at it, slamming my foot into its rocky chest but the only thing I hurt was my big toe and my pride. My vision was dimming as my brain used up the last of its oxygen. I wondered how long it would take a crushed trachea to heal when I heard Jeffrey shout out a word that sounded like, "MET!"

Suddenly I was on the ground, swimming in a mound of dusty granite and dirty Brooks Brothers suits.

Jefferey was standing above me, holding two pieces of torn parchment in each hand.

"What the hell was that?"

"A failsafe. The Hebrew word for death. Stops them cold," he said and pocketed the scraps of paper. "Get up. Something is very wrong if they are attacking me."

"You don't know the half of it."

The front door was open. I started to enter but Jeffrey pulled out his gun and pushed me to the side. I acquiesced; I had a good idea there wasn't going to be much to find.

It was worse.

David the thug was a hired gun, but he didn't deserve that.

Guessing from the dusty piles wet with blood and chunks of David, there must've been three or four golems tearing him apart when Jeffrey read from the parchment.

But I didn't have time to put together the pieces of the David puzzle.

There was a worse mess by the dining table.

What remained of Lucio Amara was on the floor. He was just a torso with a half-formed head now. Arms and legs had either been twisted off or stamped into dust. Anyone's guess was as good as anything. And did it really matter? I wasn't going to ask him for a detailed report.

His eyes flickered when I bent down beside him.

"Hello," he gasped out. "Forgive me for… not rising."

"Forgiven," I replied. "Where is Barone?"

"The bitch. Took him." Lucio's spark was waning as he struggled to talk. "Some place of power, she said. Finish the deal."

Raymond Bishop stumbled up behind Jeffrey. His face had a new crop of bruises.

"Will someone tell me what the hell just happened?" he said. "I finished zipping up and before I knew it, those stone bastards were on me, pounding me like steak and then poof! I was choking on dust…*WHAT the hell is that!*"

"Harleaux has Barone." I stood up and wiped off the grit from my pants. I didn't attempt to address the body on the floor; I just didn't have the energy.

"Wait." The word sounded like a hushed whisper.

Bishop jumped. "Holy crap, it's alive?"

"One favor."

"What?" I said.

"End this."

I nodded and stomped on his head until my shoe was ashen with dust.

"Goddamn, Jake," said Bishop. "Remind me never to ask you for a favor."

Back to the Beginning

I closed the door to the Odyssey Shop for what I thought would be the last time.

"It's going to get dangerous from here on out," I said. "If you want to back out, now's the time."

"I don't know what the hell you're on about," said Bishop. "I didn't come this far just to punk out now."

"I'm still under contract to Barone," said Jeffrey Crow. "Frankly, I'm wondering why you're still here."

"This is a fight between Harleaux and me. It ends here and now."

"Good enough for me," said Bishop.

"Now what?" said Jeffrey.

"We'll need a car," I said.

"And guns," said Bishop.

"No problem," answered Jeffrey. "Guns are easy; there are two more in the safe back in my office. Cars, even easier. We have a few out back. Wait here."

When Jeffrey went to get the guns and ammunition Bishop grabbed my arm. "We forgot about Simza. Where is she? We can't leave her behind."

I didn't know what to tell him. To be honest, I hadn't digested the truth myself. Harleaux had invaded her body and taken on her skin. Simza, no, wait... I had to say the word, if only to myself...my mother... was dead. Rage and grief intermingled. I took a deep breath and pushed back the grief. Rage was what I needed. Anger would push me forward.

I looked into his pale blue eyes. This poor bastard hadn't come down to Louisiana to confront golems or body snatching witches. He'd come down here thinking this was a simple case of a dishonest private dick duping some corn-fed farmer out of two hundred dollars. His concern for a woman he'd only known for two days was genuine and probably the only thing rooting him to reality. I couldn't take that away from him.

"Harleaux took her," I said tweaking the truth. "I have an idea where she's heading."

"More reasons to get on the road sooner than later," he said. "Let's get going, gentlemen!"

Jeffrey returned and took us around to the back of the building where a fleet of cars were parked.

It was also near the alley where Frank Weiss' body was now being bagged up by police to be escorted to the morgue. Detective Reggie Collins from homicide was flipping a lit cigarette. He looked like a dingier version of the first time we'd cross paths when Pia Lombardi broke in and "died" on my staircase: a tired man with nicotine stained teeth, in a beige suit with a tie that fit too tight.

"Wait," I said. "I know that officer."

"So what?" said Jeffrey.

"The body in the alley was a reporter on the crime beat for years. Odds are good that Collins knew Frank. On top of that, he probably knew that Frank knew Bear. I don't want to have to explain how Bear's poker buddy ended up in my back alley."

"Or the mess in the building. Got any other rides?" asked Bishop.

Jeffrey brightened up. "Yes! Mr. Barone had me stash a car down the block. It's a bucket of bolts. It's got lots of miles on it."

"We're not trying to arrive in style, kid!" said Bishop.

We dashed a block over and I've never been happier to see what Jeffrey Crowe described as a bucket of bolts.

"I'll be damned," I said.

There she was. The car Giovanna had loaned me. I left the other two behind and ran over to see if my luck would hold out for just five minutes more.

"Gentlemen, things are starting to look up." I opened the door and retrieved the red box.

"Unless that has more guns in it," said Bishop, running up beside me. "I'm not interested."

I took the lid off the box. Inside was a small blue green and red nugget that, in a hundred years, would expand and grow into a squarish ziggurat crystal, the Salt of Life.

I kissed the tiny lump and stuffed it in my pants pocket.

"Let's go," I said. "Let's end this."

"Where?" said Jeffrey. "You still haven't told us where the hell we're going."

"Back to where it began. The swamp."

CHAPTER SIXTEEN

The Lady Makes a Bomb

Harleaux's cottage hadn't fared very well in the past six months. The honeysuckle vines running around the door that had smelled so sweet six months ago had shriveled away to knobby veins.

"I found some tracks," said Jeffrey. "They lead around back. Bishop says that's where the barn is."

I cupped my hands around my face and looked through the window and felt a pull, an irresistible need to go inside.

"Hold up for a second," I said. "I need to check on something."

I pushed the door open and walked inside.

The cottage was exactly as I remembered it. A comfortable place that belied the fact it was once the home of a murdering bitch.

On the mantle over the fireplace were the photographs of her children. They were strangers to me when I first saw them six months ago but now, I could put names to two of the faces. There was her son, Theophilus. He was young, smiling, holding a diploma, and beaming with pride. It's hard to imagine that his body is now rotting in the bilge of a pirate ship deep in the swamp.

And her granddaughter, Pearl.

Damn.

I picked up her framed photograph and gently brushed away the dust from her face with my thumb. Her dark, cinnamon eyes were the same as when she asked me to put a bullet in her head. I remembered her face and her voice but not much else. The only emotion that her photograph brought was regret. I kept thinking I should feel more but I don't. Maybe something inside of me had already turned to stone.

Something fluttered and I looked up into the mirror over the mantle.

There was Simza, smiling at me.

"Oh, shit!" I looked behind me, expecting Harleaux to deliver a deathblow but I was alone.

Simza laughed silently in the mirror and cocked her finger. *Follow me.*

I followed her wispy visage as she passed by every reflective surface into the kitchen. It was a simple room with a table, wall cupboards, a sink and a three burner Westinghouse stove.

"About time you got here, Bela."

Bear was stirring a spoon in a wooden bowl. On the table beside him were several urns made from terracotta, a metal box and book bound in leather. He smiled at me and turned a page in book on the table. He looked like when I first I came to New Orleans. Barrington Gunn, the war veteran with delusions of private eye grandeur. A man who wore a fedora like others wear a badge. He was vibrant and solid. You'd never know his corpse was rotting in the barn outside.

"Looking good, Bear. Death suits you." I looked at the book he was using, expecting a cookbook, but what I got was a page full of runes and symbols that made my eyes burn. "How can you read that?"

"I don't. The Lady whispers it inside my head." Bear shivered. "Which, frankly, is creepy as hell. No offense, Lady," he said, nodding towards my mother's shadowy visage. "Look under the sink there. Get me a small jar, kid."

I found the jar. It held about an ounce and put it on the table.

"I hope to God I'm doing this right," said Bear. He held the bowl towards the stove. "How does it look?"

Simza's gauzy visage floated across the shiny oven surface. She nodded and the page of the book turned.

Inside the bowl was a pasty, curdled glob that smelled like menthol and sulfur.

"What is it?"

Bear scrapped out the glob and deposited it in the mason jar. "A bomb."

"Whoa." I stepped back.

"You don't go into a war with a feather duster, kid." Bear rolled his eyes. "Frankly, I have no idea what I'm doing. The Lady is in control, not me."

"What the hell are you doing here? I freed you."

"You did. And thanks for that. I'm here for the same reason the others are here. Revenge."

"Others?"

Bear nodded towards the stove. "Look closer."

I gazed deeper into the polished steel of Harleaux's cooking pan. They first appeared as a swirling mass, boiling and rolling until faces emerged from the cloud. It took a second for my eyes to adjust and then I saw them.

"Frank?"

Frank Weiss looked out without seeing. His eyes looked flat and hollow. I don't think he even saw me. Behind him, Onofrio Gallante looked straight at me. He definitely saw me. The hatred glowed red hot in his empty eye sockets. Behind him there were wavering shifts of light and gray. I couldn't see anyone's face. I touched the pan and the entire scene wavered like a pool of silver water.

"Yeah. There's a few others I don't know. Sad sons of bitches. Harleaux made a huge enemy when she killed the Lady." Bear laughed. "Big mistake."

"Her name is Simza," I said. "She was...is my mother."

"Wow. Now, that's a bomb," said Bear. "No wonder she's so hot about getting you here."

"Why?"

"You have the last ingredient, she says. The ignition pin, so to speak. She says it's in your..." Bear cocked his head. "Pocket?"

"What?" I pulled out the only two things I had in my pocket: my mother's protective amulet and...

"Damn."

The Seed. The last piece of the Salt of Life. My ticket that will keep me from turning into stone in a hundred years.

I clenched my fist.

"Dammit, Bear. You don't know what I've had to go through for this."

"Look, Jake, it's your choice but know this," said Bear. "Anyone that bitch has killed to use as a ride ends up in a ghost hell that is worse than being stuck in the Odyssey Shop. Ten times worse. And she'll keep on doing this until someone stands up to her. In the end, it's up to you."

Simza looked out from the shiny steel stove. Her face was blank, but I knew she was waiting to see what I'd do. Behind her, the insubstantial wraiths flailed behind her like seaweed in a rolling wave. Frank's empty eyes peeked over her shoulder. Galante glowered in the back.

"Hell." I tossed the Seed into the foul-smelling glop. There was a loud pop and the smell of sick ozone. "When has anything ever been up to me?"

"Don't get maudlin, kid. It'll give you wrinkles." Bear screwed the lid on tightly and handed me the jar.

"So, now what?"

"Wait for your opening, throw, boom. Simple as that."

"Boom?"

"Or something like that." Bear shrugged. "Look, kid, it doesn't mean much but I'm proud to have been your partner, Jake. We did good."

At that moment, the sound of heavy footsteps caught my attention. Jeff and Bishop were coming towards me from the living room.

"Where's the party?" said Bishop.

"Not here, obviously," said Jeff. "The tracks lead towards the barn."

I turned back to Bear, but he was gone. Because of course he was.

"Come on," I said. I put the jar in my coat pocket. The glass felt warm and buzzed my fingers. "There's nothing here."

We went outside in time to hear Barone's high reedy voice shout, "YOU DAMN FOOL WOMAN! THIS IS SCIENCE, NOT A PARLOUR TRICK!"

"Sounds like the party has started," I said.

We ran towards the barn. Ahead was the van that was specially equipped to hold Barone's heavy wheelchair. It was long, gray and looked like a metal tube on wheels. We stopped and used it as a shield. Crouching on the ground, our backs against the cold metal, we checked the loaded handguns Jeffrey had gotten for us. Colt .38 pistols. It made me miss my Enfield.

"Jesus," said Bishop. "What's that smell?"

The smell was a nauseating stew of burnt copper, decay and ammonia.

Being nearest to the rear wheel, I leaned over and took a peek.

And I really missed having my Enfield.

The smell was coming from Vincenzo Barone. He had been shucked from his lifesaving wheelchair and laid on the ground at Harleaux's feet. His body was a desiccated cartoon of a corpse, shriveled like beef jerky and covered in a wet black ichor.

Harleaux, wearing my mother's skin, was barely recognizable. She was taller, her arms and legs looked thinner, as were stretched on a rack. There was a ferocity burning in those eyes that belonged entirely to Harleaux. She stood over the ruined body of Barone, dangling something bundled up in a tattered cloth...

"Jake," hissed Bishop. "What's out there?"

I waved him away and tried not to breath in the stink in fear throwing up my guts and giving away our position. Right now, the element of surprise was our only ace in the hole.

"You will give me what you promised," she said and rained the macabre package over Barone. It was bones, held together by dried flesh and a tattered, burned dress. What was left of her body after the fire. "Take these and make me whole again."

"You...stupid....woman." Barone sputtered as the bones hit him on the face. "If I could give anyone a new body, wouldn't I have given myself one?"

"LIAR!" She screeched and kicked the old man, over and over. Black blood shot out of his mouth. "The Order has power. POWER TO MAKE ME WHOLE!"

The old man pleaded, "Stop! Wait! Maybe...there is another way!"

Harleaux stopped. "Keep talking."

"I can't revive your old body. That is beyond me. That is beyond anyone's power..."

"You're losing my attention, old man." Harleaux put her boot on his head and pressed his face into the mud.

"Wait! Stop! Do you like *that* body?" said Barone.

Harleaux appraised my mother's body.

"What if made *that* one immortal?"

"Interesting proposal," she said, taking her foot off his head. "I'm listening."

"That feat is within my grasp, dear lady, but first, you have to put me back into my chair and take me back to the Odyssey Shop. I have a device there that can solve both our problems. The final piece was just about to be put in place. I promise that it is only a matter of time before he acquiesces..."

I felt a hand on my shoulder.

"Simza?" Bishop tried to take a step towards her.

"ISTENHEGYI!" Harleaux roared.

"Damn!" I said and pulled him back behind the van.

"What the hell is she doing?" said Bishop. "What happened…"

Sudden realization blazed in his blue eyes.

"Simza. Back in the shop. The darkness. It won, didn't it?"

I nodded. I didn't know what to say.

And then Bishop summed it up in two words.

"That BITCH!"

"What the hell is going on, Jake?" asked Jeffrey. "What's out there?"

"Get ready to go to war, boys."

CHAPTER SEVENTEEN

RUN!

"ISTENHEGYI!" Harleaux growled and bared her teeth as she started towards me.

The bitch might wear my mother's skin but there was nothing of Simza left in that body.

I stood to face her.

"Come get it, hag," I said, reaching for the bomb.

"No! Stop, you stupid woman!" Barone yelled, his ruined body wriggled in frustration. "Istenhegyi is the final component of the device. His blood is the key to immortality!"

"Well, I really hate to ruin your plans," I cocked my hand back, readying to toss the jar like a football. "But this ends now."

Harleaux waved her hand and an invisible force slammed against my arm. The jar flipped from my fingers, arced, and fell short, crashing against the head of Vicenzo Barone.

"Dammit!"

"What is this?" Barone spat out the goop. "What is...oh...oh....no...no...NO!"

The screams started just as the grayish goop turned black and grew, mushrooming all over Barone's body.

Jeffrey Crowe stood at attention as he heard his boss cry out but stopped and stayed behind me, shaking his head.

There was nothing we can do.

"What is this?" Harleaux said as she shrank away from the monster growing in front of her. "What dark magic is this?"

The goop grew skyward, arcing upwards like a volcanic plume. Barone's skeletal figure was pulled upwards, twisting and turning, as it slowly solidified into stone. Parts of him jutted out all along the column. An arm. A leg. An ear. His face, trapped in a painful grimace, capped the top like a grotesque totem pole.

"Mr. Barone?" Jeffrey said as he walks towards his employer.

Barone's eyes rolled towards the sound of his name.

"He's still alive!" Jeffrey raised his gun towards the horror. "Oh my God! He's still alive!"

He did Barone a kindness and shot bullet after bullet into the tower of stone.

"NO!" Harleaux leaped and wrestled Jeffrey to the ground. She held him down as she clawed at him like a wildcat. "You bastard! He was my only hope. My only hope!"

Bishop and I ran to Jeffrey just as Harleaux bit into his neck. Blood spurted out as she twisted her head, mangling the flesh and ripping out his windpipe.

"Jesus!" Bishop skidded to a dead stop, falling down on his ass and taking me down with him.

"Ahhh! Istenhegyi!" Harleaux turned towards us, crawling on all fours, her snarling face a smearing of gore and blood. "I will have you next!"

"You have to catch me first! Run, Bishop, RUN!"

Adrenaline gave my legs extra power and I was able to get up and start running away, pulling Bishop along with me.

CHAPTER EIGHTEEN

Calling an Old Friend

The swamp in the winter was a different place. The bald limbs of the cypress trees looked like skeletal claws reaching up to the sky. The stink was deeper but lower as if the cold air pushed it down.

All in all, I was still grateful for the lack of chickens.

Bishop and I ran until we came to the cold, marshy swampland. Somewhere, I didn't have the guts to look, the screams of the monster Henrietta Harleaux echoed behind us.

"Wait, wait, WAIT!" Bishop grabbed my arm and pulled me to a stop. "Damn, I hate running." Bishop growled. "Tell me you've got a plan."

"I have an idea." I said, bent over, huffing, trying to get my breath back. "It's a long shot but it's our only shot."

"As long as one of us does."

I didn't have the heart to tell Bishop how long a shot it was.

"Let's go," I said. "We need to go deeper."

"Deeper? Jesus, the only thing out there are alligators, rats, and God knows what else!"

"Let's pray you're right." I walked into the marshy wetland until I was up to my knees. I sank into the mud and my shoes quickly filled with thick muck. "Do you have a pocketknife?"

"I think so." Bishop searched his pockets and tossed me his knife. "Why?"

"Calling an old friend." I opened the knife and slashed it across my palm. I squatted and thrust my bloody hand into the mud. "Pray this works."

Harleaux appeared from behind a cypress tree.

"That's a good way to get a nasty infection, Istenhegyi."

It was as if she pulled herself from out of the bark of the tree. Her neck had grown more vertebrae and her five fingers had melded into three giving her hands a talon. She looked like a human caricature of the monster snake god I had killed only six months earlier.

"Bishop, run!" I said.

Bishop, much to his credit, didn't ask any questions, or make a smartass bon mot and simply ran.

Unfortunately, not quickly enough.

She waved a gnarled talon at him and the sharp claw shot off, slammed into his shoulder and nailed him to the ground.

"Stay, boy," she smirked. "I'll deal with you later. But, first…Istenhegyi, now you will be mine!"

CHAPTER NINETEEN

Around and Around Again

So, here I am, up to my elbows in swamp muck, staring down a body hopping witch who wants to kill me. Not the way I wanted to start the new year.

"Do you want to know what I'm going to do to you first?" she croaked.

Harleaux takes a step forward, the muck swallowing her shoe. She lets out a long hiss and her head cocks unnaturally to one side. "I will slice your skin off in strips and then watch it slowly grow back just so I can rip it off again. I'm going to strap you down, cut off pieces and watch it grow back. I'm going to burn you to a crisp, watch you heal, peel off your skin, and boil you. I am going to listen to you scream and beg me to stop."

"Well, that is very specific," I say, smiling despite the dryness of my mouth. "You've put a lot of thought into this, I can tell."

"You ruined my life, Istenhegyi. I am going to destroy yours."

She takes another step forward. There is a rumbling beneath my feet.

"But, for now," she says, her lips pull into a psychotic grin. "I'll settle for slicing off your face."

She screams a shrill cry and slashes her razor-sharp claw hand towards me just as a thick green wall erupts between us.

"Yes!' I shout in victory as the Boodaddy answers my call and creates a hedgerow fortress wall of kudzu, mud and swamp detritus.

"You son of a bitch!" she cries. "You can't hide from me behind your swamp monster!"

The wall shudders as she claws at the Boodaddy like hedge clippers. Inside the brown sludge, I see the dark empty eye sockets of a mummified skull.

Henrietta Harleaux's skull.

I pluck it out just as the wall falls into the swamp.

I hold it above my head and command, "Henrietta Harleaux, I command you return to your skull!"

Harleaux laughs. "What? HAHAHA! Oh, you stupid, insane, boy! You think you can command me? *Here?* You are in my spiritus loci. You have no power here."

"True," I say. "But they do."

I point to the gathering of shades behind her. My mother, Frank and Galante at the front of the crowd. In a motion faster than my eye could follow, the gang of shades attacks. Harleaux flails her long, spider like arms, swatting the spirits of her dead victims like flies.

"No, no, no, NO! Get away!" She slaps at the shades as they swarm around her.

In the water around me, the Boodaddy pulls itself together into the crude shape of a man. A veiny arm swipes the skull from my hand and another hand shoots vines out at Harleaux as it attempts to pull her into itself.

She slashes back at the veins with her talons, cutting through them.

At that moment, Bear Gunn appears to Henrietta Harleaux.

"You!" she cries out.

"You remember me? I'm touched." he says. "While I don't normally advocate hitting a woman, in your case, I'll let this one slide."

Bear punches Harleaux in the jaw, sending her backwards into the Boodaddy. It wraps kudzu vines around her body, cocooning her thrashing frame until there is a sharp crack as it snaps her neck.

"Go back to hell, bitch." Bear growls and the eyes of the skull glows as Henrietta Harleaux finds her way back home.

I look into the empty eye sockets and see her inside, screaming in rage.

Satisfied, I tell the Boodaddy to go back to the swamp.

"Take it far away. Never let it see the light of day again."

The creature shivers and disappears as it melts into the wetland.

The shades of Simza, Frank and Galante stand beside Bear. They look as solid as he does and they slowly blink away, crossing over to wherever the dead finally rest.

Simza blows me a kiss before she disappears into a ball of light.

Bear salutes me and says, "See you on the other side, kid."

And I am left alone.

Until I remember Bishop.

I run over to him and remove the claw that pins him down like a butterfly to a board.

"You okay?"

Bishop sits up, rubbing his shoulder and nods. "I think so. I'm just wondering how the hell I'm going to write this up in a report!"

CHAPTER TWENTY

Burning Bridges

It was near midnight when Bishop and I made it back to the Odyssey Shop. There was no moon. Exactly what we needed to complete the job.

We spent an hour in the utility room smashing the sarcophagi into bits and drenching it in kerosene.

Then we took the rest of the night to fully soak the entire building in gasoline, kerosene, bottles of whiskey, hell, anything we could find that would burn.

"You sure you want to do this?" said Bishop.

"I've never been surer of anything in my life," I said. "Some bridges deserve to be burned."

By the time the sound of the firetruck sirens could be heard, Bishop and I were blocks away in one of the cars left behind by the now definitely late, but not so great, Vicenzo Barone.

"Are you worried about repercussions? Won't there be questions?" asked Bishop.

"With any luck they'll think Dave's burned body is mine. That's what I'm hoping for. Time to start over."

"Good luck with that," he said. "What's your plan now?"

"I need to find another seed crystal of the Salt of Life, but I've got decades to worry about that. Right now, I've got unfinished business with my thieving half-brother in Los Angeles."

"Los Angeles? That's my stomping ground."

"He stole a fortune in gold, and I want it back."

"Oh yeah? Looking for a partner?"

"Depends. Can I bum a ride?"

The End

A QUICK NOTE:

The next two chapters are a quick teaser of the 7th book in Jake's saga.

It's been a long, weird trip writing Jake's story. It's like driving on a dark, winding road, in the fog, with weak headlights. I have an idea of what might be in front of me.

Or it might be a cliff.

Let's find out together.

JAKE ISTENHEGYI:

THE ACCIDENTAL DETECTIVE

Guns,

Gold,

With a Dash of

Glamour

I dedicate this to the Readers.

Thanks for coming along for the ride.

Now, buckle up.

This is going to get bumpy.

CHAPTER ONE

Welcome to Hollywood

A golden laurel ring weaves through the singer's jet-black hair. His clenched hands are reaching skyward as his voice reaches higher and higher.

And then the stretched-out note becomes a scream.

The wax I stuffed earlier today in my ears is the only thing keeping me alive.

Too bad the bastards I'm stepping over didn't get the memo.

The thrum of the sound vibrates through the floors, shoots up my legs and into drills into my spine. Lights fall from the ceiling like shooting stars and the fake walls painted to look like frescoes of a brothel in Pompeii fall over like dominoes.

Above the singer, there is a rip in the sky.

I wish I could say it was fake.

Something purple begins to bleed through, flashing a freezing light first around the singer and then spreading like a cancer slowly across the floor.

And, yet the Singer stays on key.

He deserves praise for that, at least.

If he wasn't ending the world, that is.

I take a deep breath and aim my snub nose at the stupid bastard's forehead. One shot to save everything.

My name is Jake Istenhegyi. And this is one hell of a family reunion.

CHAPTER TWO

Starting Over

We left the blazing hulk of the Odyssey Shop and drove for hours in silence. Bishop stared ahead, his hands turning white with a death grip on the steering wheel.

I just kept looking out the window, flipping my mother's coin across my knuckles. I didn't want to talk. I needed to think and figure out what to do next. If things went smoothly, everyone would think that one of the bodies left behind in the fire was mine.

I could start over.

New life. New name. Something that wasn't such a tongue twister as Istenhegyi.

And when I found Radu and got my gold back, I'd be able to do it in style.

Until then, I practiced flipping my mother's coin across my knuckles and tried to avoid Bishop's glares.

The tension finally broke in Houston.

Raymond Bishop, a private detective from L.A. who, a few days ago, was just a guy on a routine case, chasing down some deadbeat who ran off with his client's money only to find himself confronted with golems, swamp monsters, undead alchemists and body switching witches, finally lost it.

He pulled off the road, skidding to a stop. "Hell!" he said, slamming his fist on the steering wheel.

"Problem?"

"What the hell happened back there, Jake? I mean…what…I was there…I saw it…but…WHAT THE HELL?"

"What part didn't you understand? The undead alchemists that wanted to create an elixir from my blood? The swamp monster that saved our asses at the last minute? The ghosts? The man who literally turned into sand in front of your eyes? Should I continue?"

Bishop shook his head. "It was true then? All of it?"

"Look, I get it. Seven months ago, I was just kid playing detective with my best friend. Today, I'm an immortal shmuck running off to Los Angeles to get back the pirate treasure stolen by his gypsy half-brother. Welcome to my world."

Bishop pulled back onto the road. "I still don't know how I'm going to write this up in a report. No one is going to believe it. They are going to put me in a looney bin or worse!"

We drove for another twelve hours only stopping over in New Mexico to visit with Giovanna Lombardi-Bonham.

She lived with her son, Arthur, in a home that was crafted by her late husband, Archibald. It was a Spanish adobe style building with a flat Mission Revival styled roof, tiles of sunburnt clay, pinkish white walls with wooden dowels jutting out every foot and circular windows. It butted up against a hillside dotted with scrub grass until the two were indistinguishable.

The last time I saw her, she gave me a newly created crystal seed that would eventually grow into the Sal Vitae Aeternam. The Salt of Life. The vital ingredient to the elixir that I would need to drink every hundred years to avoid turning into stone.

And I used it to make a bomb to kill a monster.

When I stop to think about how ludicrous my life has become…

We arrived early in the evening. I don't even know what day it was, but we were greeted with open arms.

Bishop barely made it to the guest room before he collapsed.

I was tired but seeing her gave me a boost that I needed more than sleep. She looked so radiant, so alive. I wanted to stay awake just to be with her.

"Sorry about not calling first," I said.

"Don't be silly," she said, leading me to the living room. "You are family. Our doors are always open to you and your friends."

"Arthur looks…fit. More color to his face than last time I saw him."

"He will heal in time; God knows we have plenty of it. He still has nightmares. I don't want to think about what tortures those bastards put him through in the years they had him hostage."

"Well, about that…"

The hours slipped by as we ate, drank wine and I told her about everything that had happened in New Orleans. The end of the Odyssey Shop. The final death of Bear. My mother. The news about Lucio. She didn't need to worry about the Order of Zosimos; everyone was dead. For real, this time. There was no coming back for any of them.

"And so is Jake Istenhegyi," she said.

"Yeah, I guess so. That part hasn't really sunk in yet. You did say that I would have to change my identity eventually."

"Every thirty or forty years, is the rule of thumb,

yes. One of the very annoying realities that helps keep us safe."

"I guess Los Angeles is a good enough place to be reborn."

"Yes, I suppose." Giovanna took a drink, her lips lingering on the rim of the glass. "Or you could stay here. With us. We can work together on creating a new seed crystal. You'd be safe here. We can be family."

Bishop walked in, chewing on a chicken leg. "Hey, buddy. Ready to get back on the road?"

Giovanna looked at me, wondering. "Are you?"

"I have to," I said. "I've spent my entire life being shuffled around, hidden, living on the largess of others." A lightbulb went off inside my head. "Jesus, I just realized that. This is the first time in my life I'm really on my own."

"So be it." Giovanna smiled but the sadness behind her eyes betrayed her. "You're growing up, Jake Whoever-You-Are-Now. So, go. Come back with more stories and adventures. Don't be a stranger."

We stood and I held her, whispering in her ear, "I'll be back."

Those words were still ringing in my ears four days later when we finally made it to Los Angeles.

Raymond Bishop lived in a second story apartment that would've made Mama Effie rolled her eyes. One large room that held a couch, a cigarette scarred coffee table, a radio that perched hazardously on the windowsill, and a carpet that had met a Hoover. A diploma, awards for public heroism in the line of duty as a policeman, and yellowed newspaper articles were tacked to the wall. A display Bear would've called an "I Love Me" wall.

Damn. I missed them.

A bedroom doglegged off the left of main room and through some pocket doors on the right was a small kitchen with an icebox and hotplate. Two cups, two plates, two bowls were all the dishes Bishop owned.

"Expecting company?" I asked.

"No. That way I only have to wash dishes every other day." He tapped his forehead. "Smart, see?"

Bishop left hours ago to file his case report with his boss. His boss was expecting either their client's money back or some idea where their son could be found. I can't imagine what he wrote. "Well, you see, I followed all the evidence and they led me to a shack in the bayou and, well, yadda, yadda, everybody's dead."

Yeah, that should go over well.

I sat on the couch, watching some daredevils across the street hang up a movie poster on the brick wall. One man would slather glue on the bricks with what looked like a paint roller with a twelve-foot handle. The second man would carefully balance a strip of canvas on a long horizontal metal ledge, slap it onto the gooey stuff and quickly flatten and level it at the same time. It was mesmerizing. I let it ease my mind as I flipped Simza's coin over and over, one knuckle at a time, thinking.

How the hell was I going to find Radu? He could be anywhere. Where to even begin?

The door slammed and broke my train of thought.

"SONS OF BITCHES!"

"Bad day at the office, dear?"

"They fired me. Sacked me. Not only that, they took expenses out of my final check. Sons of bitches!"

"Hmmm."

"No justice in this world," he said, throwing himself down on the couch beside me. He looks deflated and defeated. "None! Sons of bitches! Now what am I going to do?"

Inspiration struck.

"Looks like you need a job."

"No shit, Sherlock."

"How about me? What if I hired you? To help me find Radu and get my gold back."

Bishop looked at me with his hard, pale blue eyes. "I'm listening."

"I can't pay you-"

"Well, hells bells, how does that help me?!"

"Listen, I can't pay you *now* but once we find Radu and get the gold, I'll give you ten percent."

"Fifteen," he said.

"Fine." I was never good at haggling.

"It's a deal then," he said.

Bishop stood and started pacing. "Okay, you said he came to Los Angeles to become a movie star, right? So, I have friends in Hollywood who can check out some studio lots, look for some new faces. I can also pull in some favors from some buds that work that beat. Maybe he's ended up in the clink?"

As he paced back and forth, his voice faded into the background as my eyes went back to the open window and the men outside putting up a movie poster. They had finished with the third and final panel.

"What the hell?"

"What?"

I pointed at the poster.

Colossal letters in red and gold screamed, THE GOLDEN HOUR! Below it was the tagline: *His passion could bend any woman to his will!* A beautiful woman, her svelte, nearly nude body gracefully swooned over a golden altar. Above her, a ruthlessly handsome man in a torn shirt stared out of the poster with a leering smile. Starring COLLEEN STARR! JAKE POWELL!

"I think I found a lead."

TO BE CONTINUED....

ABOUT THE AUTHOR

Nikki Nelson-Hicks lives in a small room and leaves behind too many empty wine glasses for one person.

Please check out her Amazon author page:
amazon.com/author/nikkinelsonhicks